The Last Word

Also by Mark Illis

Tender (Salt)
A Chinese Summer (Bloomsbury)
The Alchemist (Bloomsbury)
The Feather Report (Bloomsbury)

The Last
Word

MARK ILLIS

SALT

LONDON

PUBLISHED BY SALT PUBLISHING

Acre House, 11-15 William Road, London NW1 3ER United Kingdom

© Mark Illis, 2011

Printed in Great Britain by Clays Ltd, St Ives plc

Typeset in Bembo 12 / 13.5

ISBN 978-1-907773-09-9 paperback

1 3 5 7 9 8 6 4 2

For Dean

Thursday

Departure

THE NEWS CAME by phone. He asked if he was talking to Gloria. I said yes. He said, 'Gloria Rumat?' I said yes. He said he was Stephen, calling from England, and he had bad news. His voice was very quiet, and I asked him to speak up. He told me my brother had died. He paused, and so did I. I felt I'd been rattled, picked up and shaken. Silence between us for a few seconds. The soft hush of distance on the phone line, my unsteady breathing. I asked him how Max had died, and he said he'd fallen under a train. Barely audible. I didn't know if it was him whispering or a fault on the line. I said, 'Did he fall or did he jump?' Stephen murmured that he fell.

My mother always hated the phone. She seldom answered it, said it was an intrusion, no better than someone bellowing at you through your letterbox. That was my first thought, my hand still resting lightly on the receiver. There was an image in my head of Stephen crouching outside my front door, shouting quietly. Then I started to feel loose and liquid. I slopped from one side of the flat to the other, stared out of the window, sat down and looked for a long time at my knees. The textures of things attracted my fingers. They moved slowly over the cushion beside me. Small soft bristles, moving back-wards and forwards. I stood abruptly, went to the kitchen and hovered somewhere behind my shoulder, watching myself find a mug, a teabag. I put them down, held on to the counter and gripped it, weeping.

Then the process of leaving. The big, thin-walled space of the airport, the feeling of unburdening when my bag was checked in, all the journeys swimming around me, about to start. Through Passport Control, through the spindly door-frame of the metal detector, and into the Departure Lounge.

I bought a coffee, sat at a plastic table, watched the monitor. *Wait in lounge.* I'd spent a year in Hong Kong, but it felt like I'd arrived the previous week, and the intervening time had been compressed into a few days. Teaching English, going to the races, sailing in the harbour, brief trips into mainland China, meeting Clara. I sipped coffee, scratched at a brown stain on the dimpled surface of the table. It felt like everywhere I'd been was the Departure Lounge. A comfortable space, with food-stops and things to do, but not a destination, not a settled *place*.

Scratching the stain had left brown stuff under my fingernail, dried coffee. I used the stirrer to dislodge it, then scratched some more. I'd met Clara at the races soon after I arrived. She'd come up and asked my advice on a horse. I told her I had no idea. She looked a bit taken aback by my tone; not angry, just puzzled. Usually I'd have walked away, but I found myself feeling sorry. Perhaps it was her puzzlement, perhaps the unlikely white cardigan she was wearing. I said I preferred cats to horses. She stared at me a second, then laughed, and we made a bet together, then had a drink together, and soon found that we'd spent the day together.

Without noticing what I was doing, I'd scratched an *M* into the stain on the table. M for Max. I studied the letter until it was just a shape, a house with the roof fallen in, then finished my soapy coffee. No one in miles of where I was sitting knew I was bereaved. That didn't seem right. The businesswoman at the next table pressed a key on her laptop and gave a satisfied grunt. She was wearing a sleeveless red top and her left hand was stroking her temple. She looked like she belonged in an advert. I felt like tapping her on the shoulder, telling her my brother had just died.

I stared at her, then stood, went over, and tapped her on the shoulder.

She looked up, a frown falling across her face. 'Yes?'

I hesitated. Saw the wariness in her eyes as she gauged how much trouble I was going to be.

'Nothing. Sorry.'

I returned to my table. Watched the monitor.

Clara came round soon after the phone call. 'Jesus, Gloria,' she said, and hugged me. I smelt her hair, felt her jumper against my cheek, let her keep her arms tight round me while I shed some tears on her shoulder.

She took me out and we wandered for a while, found ourselves on Nathan Road and visited the jade market, where grinning men tried to push bangles and rings on us. I shook my head, 'No, no, no thanks,' like an uneasy tourist again, on her first day on the island. Clara took control, put her arm in mine and took me to a café where she had a bowl of soup and I smoked cigarettes and drank green tea.

I didn't want to talk about Max, so we talked about my plans instead. How strange it was, after a year in Hong Kong, to be reeled back, across half the world, back to a small town in Yorkshire. I said, 'I can't stay in England, I don't know anyone there.' She tried to interrupt but I over-rode her. 'No, I need my life peopled. I like saying

I'm having drinks with you on Tuesday, seeing a film with Joe on Friday, going to that club on Saturday. I need it peopled and I need it thing-ed. There's that thing on Tuesday, another on Friday, and that thing on Saturday. I can't stay in England, I can't be where I don't know anyone.'

I had a feeling I might be gabbling. If I was Clara I'd have been tempted to slap me, but she was calmly finishing her soup, tipping a morsel of crab meat on to her spoon. I was grateful to her. In every area where I floundered she was competent. She wasn't very good at boyfriends or clothes, but in the adult areas of life she excelled. Her work was well paid and had prospects; she had cultivated a social life; she thought about the future; and now it seemed she knew how to cope with a bereaved friend.

'You'll meet people in England,' she said, slow and unruffled. 'You shouldn't come straight back. You should stay.'

This was an old argument. I'd told her many times that I made friends rarely, and flukily. 'I won't meet anyone,' I said. 'I'm terrible at meeting people.'

The stain had almost gone, just a ghost of an outline left, and a little pile of flaky brown matter. Still twenty minutes to spend in the Lounge. I felt already out of Hong Kong, but not yet anywhere else.

I found a seat near another monitor. In the next row a Chinese man was sitting erect, looking sombrely into space. Wrinkled brown skin, brown suit, black tie. He had an urn on his lap. I stared. An urn? Surely there'd be rules about that sort of thing. Was he going to carry ashes on his lap in the plane? It was a cream-coloured, curvy little urn, plastic, I thought. If you were in a supermarket, you'd expect it to contain a milkshake.

Casual but direct, I approached, hovered, and sat down beside him. The tulip seat sloped, cupping my hips. After a moment, I glanced down at his lap, and held the look, hoping for a spontaneous reaction from him, to ease me into conversation. *Ah, I see you're looking at my urn.* Something like that. He kept gazing elsewhere. Normally, I'd have left him to it. Normally, I'd have felt he had a right to his privacy, but at this moment I felt we were members of a club. That was the spirit, camaraderie, not nosiness.

I was about to speak, on the brink of it, when, with a little wet sound from inside his mouth, he stood up suddenly and marched off. I stood up too, angry, about to follow and grab his shoulder — *How dare he?* I stopped myself. I watched him walk on, not knowing I'd moved, and then I sat down again, casual, as if nothing had happened. I was furious with myself. I hadn't wanted to upset him, I just wanted to talk to somebody who might understand. Perhaps I'd email Clara about it later. *See? Terrible at meeting people.*

I was probably better on my own anyway, because this was a natural point to start thinking about Max, this quiet point after all the hasty business of the last few days. But I didn't. Didn't think about Max. My hand lay on my bag, as if I was protecting it. Snubbed, touching my bag, people-watching, I sat there, not really in Hong Kong, but not yet anywhere else. Breathing in and breathing out, fast and shallow, as if I'd recently finished a race.

And now the monitor said I had two hours to wait. Moments ago, it was twenty minutes. What had happened to time?

Trying to be pragmatic and calm, I reviewed my itinerary. If my flight was not further delayed I would just make it to the funeral, jet-lagged and ragged, at midday on Friday. Then, Clara had said, I'd probably need some time to 'sort things out' before I came back. Who knows, she'd said, maybe I'd decide to stay.

'No,' I insisted. 'There's the life I've got here—some friends, a job, everything I need. Or there's England—no friends, no job, no Max. I like it here, I like it here, I like it here.' I was slapping the table in front of me. Bereavement seemed to have made me more emphatic.

'OK.' Clara's tone was gentle, like she was soothing an anxious pet. 'I'm just saying, you're a bit at the edge of things here, and this could be an opportunity.'

'I hate opportunities. Everything's fine, and then an opportunity comes along and you have to think about changing it all. Maybe I like being at the edge of things. Have you thought of that?'

'Do you?'

'Of course not.'

I look at people who aren't at the edge of things, who confidently occupy the centre, and I admire them. Like Clara, working at the bank and earning a stash of money to take back to England in her planned and sensible way. Navigating a steady path through her life. When I look at her, I feel precarious.

An hour had passed, it was already past midnight, but the monitor now told me I had three more hours to wait. Time was definitely acting up. I looked at my watch, made some calculations. I was tired and disorientated, it wasn't easy to work out the maths, but it was pretty obvious that I was going to miss Max's funeral.

I'm going to miss my brother's funeral. The thought started to buzz in my head. I felt raw, and tender. Might they hurry everything up, if I told them about Max? I imagined a delay caused by terrorists, frantic behind-the-scenes activity, a bomb, things flying apart. The whole airport felt unsolid, it was easy to imagine it all floating away in pieces.

I climbed on my seat. It was something to do with wondering if I could see the gate from where I was, or even the plane. There was nothing different to see except the tops of heads, but I stayed there, as people started to stare. It gets on my nerves when people stare, so puzzled or worried by any rupture in the normal way things happen. I wanted to shout: 'I'm going to miss my brother's funeral!' but I didn't. I just stood there, on my seat, until eventually people looked away, realising that nothing exciting was going to happen. Then I stood there some more, to make it clear I wasn't being intimidated. Then I sat down.

Paint

STEPHEN CLOSED HIS eyes a moment, thinking of Max. He took a deep breath. Warm, grass-scented air, traffic-sounds, the excited yelps of kids on the brink of summer.

'All right, Mr Palmer?'

He opened his eyes, looked blankly at Janice Shaw, then nodded. Usually he'd have grinned, come out with a joke, but he found he couldn't muster a smile. He looked at the children around him. The game of rounders had paused, only a couple of competitive boys had been engaged by it.

'Come on,' he said. 'Let's go in.' There were shouts as they ran for the door. 'Calm down,' he called, as they barged and squealed. 'Take your time.'

Good advice for life. Something to help these children when they walked into the sprawling comprehensive in September, to see them through into adolescence, and beyond. What did Mr Palmer say? Calm down and take your time. Thirty-one eleven-year-olds made their way into the classroom, fidgeting, shuffling and chattering, waiting for the bell to mark the end of term, the end of primary school. Stephen groped for words to match the significance of the moment.

'You've been . . .' he began.

What had they been? He'd enjoyed his year with them. He'd helped Jake through the crisis with his mother,

Angie was perhaps less of a bully than she'd been in September, they generally seemed to like him and had learnt a certain amount from him. There were nine cards on his desk. THANK YOU. Floral designs. All from girls. Thirty-one faces looked up at him, waiting for him to finish his sentence. Fortunately, one of them spoke.

'What are you going to do this summer?'

Stephen looked at the inquisitive girl. Ella. She'd been asking questions all year long. 'What am I going to do?'

Ella nodded.

He gave it a moment's thought, and came up with no ideas. He'd been focused recently on the funeral, and hadn't thought beyond it. *Bury my best friend*, he didn't say. 'Each holiday,' he did say, 'I try to do something brand new. I suggest you all do the same.'

'I'm going to Spain,' said Ella.

'Anyway, thank you,' Stephen was addressing them all, for the last time. 'And good luck. Good luck in the future.'

The bell went before the next question could come, and he watched them rise from their tables again, like plants on a speeded-up nature film. He said good bye several times and good luck, raised a hand, smiled and nodded, smiled and nodded, and watched them cramming themselves through the door, rushing off into the last summer before their new lives surprised them. He remained seated until the last of them had gone, and then remained seated some more, as the sounds of the day slowly vanished around him.

Thank you to a speshal teacher. He stared at the card, thinking about his email from Gloria. *Hope you can accomodate me a night or two*. He'd been good at spelling at school, only got into trouble once, when he drew a picture of a tank between questions during a test. He'd shown the picture to the friend sitting next to him, and Miss Glenn had accused him of cheating. She believed him though, when he told her what had happened. That was how it went in those days: problems seemed enormous, but were fairly easy to resolve. These days problems seemed enormous, and it turned out that they were.

He'd stared at that *accomodate*, trying to glean something from it. He was aware that it was petty to notice a spelling mistake in the face of death, but he liked to think that if he got the syntax of a sentence right, other things might naturally follow. The syntax of events, the whole chain of them that make up a life.

Rachel came in ten minutes later, while he was clearing up. She said nothing, just watched him. He was in the Craft Corner, putting lids on pots of paint. He continued, pretending he hadn't noticed her. If he'd been explaining to the children the meaning of the word *unnerving*, he might have described a situation like this. After some seconds he turned round.

'Look,' he tried, 'you and I shouldn't be like this, we should be . . .'

Her stare was like a physical thing, it stopped up his mouth.

'Yes?' she said.

'I was going to say friendly.'

They'd been friendly until recently. When Stephen arrived at the school in the autumn he'd noticed Rachel, because it was hard not to. Corkscrew curls and bright red lipstick. Big teeth. Too big actually, and a slightly gummy smile, but what put him off was her self-absorption. Every subject, food, scuba-diving, the *Godfather* films, seemed to find its way back to her. It made him feel inadequate, as if he was failing to contribute his share to the conversation. Four months after they'd first kissed, he'd dumped her, over a meal in the Thai restaurant. She asked why, he was evasive, and with a talent for melodrama he should have predicted, she threw a glass of wine in his face and walked out. Hard to carry that off coolly, when the waiter's looking disdainful and the couple at the next table are smirking.

'*Friendly*,' she sneered.

He shrugged. 'Fine, forget it. What do you want?'

'I just came to look.'

He'd been thinking at one stage of compiling a book of rejection stories. He'd rejected a few women in the past couple of years, and before that he'd had one unforgettable experience of being rejected, with Jude.

He wiped up a puddle of paint, aware of her still there, still looking. She wore a red skirt, white shirt, brown suede waistcoat. He'd liked the feel of that waistcoat, he'd liked to mould it around her and to rub his own bare skin against it. Physically, they'd fitted well, but he didn't want to think about that so he self-consciously, under her gaze, washed brushes.

'Sorry you're being like this,' he said, watching green paint cloud into a jar of water.

When he looked round, she'd gone.

Leaving, he did the deep sighing Max had taught him, filling his chest, shrugging his shoulders in the car seat, hoping that he could slough off Rachel's hostility. He paused at a junction, waiting for a space. Rachel was all he needed, with death so prominent in his mind. He felt a welcome pulse of anger. What was she doing, giving him a hard time the day before the funeral? He should have been tougher with her. He tried out a few lines he could have used, spoke them out loud, but none of them were smart enough. Perhaps he should have avoided speech and thrown paint at her, red of course, in a splatter over her shirt. That would have shocked her. She'd probably have picked up some yellow, because yellow is her favourite colour, and thrown it at him. He found himself smiling. He could feel the weight of the big can in his hands, he could see the wave of paint looping towards her. Wet, sticky, colourful, like characters in a piece of slapstick. Where would they have gone from there?

He was pondering — rage or laughter, sex in the stationery cupboard or never speaking to each other again — he was pondering when a horn blared behind him. He drove on. He wasn't a paint thrower, he'd have to be a different person to throw paint, more like Rachel, more like Max for that matter.

At the next lights, he watched a kid receiving a cornet from a man bending deeply out of the window of his van. The boy took it, reaching up his money at the same time, and somehow during the exchange the ice-cream tipped, slid off the cone, and slupped on to the pavement. It lay there in a little mound, like an outcrop of fungus. The lights changed and Stephen turned left and accelerated away. He was in the kind of mood to notice small events, to find significance in them. This one was not auspicious, but perhaps the man would generously offer another cornet. He preferred to imagine that and drive away, rather than wait for whatever might happen next.

Ice-cream was on his mind now. At home, he dropped his bag and crouched in the kitchen in front of the freezer. It blew cold air over him as he extracted a frost-rimed half-empty tub. *Cookies and Cream*. Stabbed a spoon into it. He made only a tiny indentation, so wrapped his palms round the tub as if praying, and carried it with him. When he'd had cold hands in bed, Rachel had squeezed them under her arm-pit or between her thighs. Jude had told him to warm them.

There were two bills, and a letter. He took the letter and the ice-cream upstairs with him, undressed and started a bath, turning the hot tap full on. Water drooled out sluggishly. A problem with the plumbing.

Naked, a bath running, ice-cream tempering, the summer holiday ahead. These are the ingredients of a good mood. He wished he could feel better than this. A movement caught his eye, and he turned, saw his reflection. He thought of the actor who spots his face in the mirror when he hears his mother has died. He pauses and examines it to see what bereavement looks like. Stephen paused, and examined. Just the usual bags under his eyes, a droopiness around the mouth. A flatness about his gaze. He squeezed out a smile, and then watched it empty from his face as his muscles relaxed.

Leaving the ice-cream in the steam, he crossed the landing, and entered Max's room. Didn't look around, had no impulse to explore, just sat at the desk and picked up Max's last piece. It was a polished, honey-coloured wooden box, as long as his hand, like a miniature, doorless cabinet. It was inlaid with a delicate silver tracery that spiralled around it like a climbing vine.

The box was light, clearly hollow, but Stephen could find no catch or opening in it. It still had a faint, sweet smell of varnish. And when he shook it, there was a sound, a tapping like a playing card tapped on a table.

Max had left something in there. A note. Stephen stared at the box, as if it might give up its secret in pure embarrassment, turned it, stroked it, then replaced it on the desk.

He opened his post and unfolded the letter inside.

So now what are you going to do?
Your best friend's dead, what next?
You could start by telling the truth,
that would be novel.
And Stephen, by the way,
you're a disaster with women.
Don't know why, don't know what it is,
but you're a disaster.

He stared at it blankly, shaking his head. He was shivering, and it was only partly because he was naked. He screwed up the note, furious, clenched it in his fist, then reluctantly, as if someone else was moving his fingers, he opened his hand and gently unpeeled the tight ball of paper, flattening it on Max's desk. Now the note was a map, crazily scribbled by roads. He took it into the bathroom.

What are you going to do this summer? He wanted, without causing any damage, to find a way into Max's piece and read the note he'd left. He dug his spoon into a white boulder of ice-cream, mottled with chocolate and biscuit, and gasped as it slid off the spoon on to his tongue. He didn't want some vague sign from Max, he wanted a clear message from one friend to another. That would make an anonymous letter irrelevant.

But who could have sent it? Who would do that to him?

Soon, Max's sister would arrive. Gloria. He knew nothing about her, but he suspected she might try to take away Max's belongings. Perhaps he should have some paint ready, in case of arguments. He slid into the filling bath feet first, as if into a sleeping bag, still holding the letter. He read it again, out loud, in a whisper that began to tremble before he reached the end.

Friday

Boundaries

WE LIFTED OFF the world, and I imagined not ever setting down again.

Clara had given me a list. She said I should take a book and a magazine, and a cushion for my neck. She said, 'Get up and walk around every hour, so the blood doesn't collect in your ankles.' Don't drink alcohol. Do drink water. Sleep as much as you can. Book an aisle seat. Don't talk to whoever's next to you. Do exercises in the loo. Take toothpaste.

I listened to her. I did my smiling, nodding, slightly glazed thing. I had no book or magazine, no neck-cushion, no intention of standing up, and every intention of drinking alcohol. I didn't feel like sleeping, or doing exercises, I hadn't booked an aisle seat, and my toothpaste was in my bathroom in my little tower-block apartment which was now receding at six hundred miles an hour. However, I had managed not to talk to the fat American sitting next to me, even though he'd asked my name, and asked if I was all right. I'd had two goes at talking to strangers in the airport, and it hadn't worked. I didn't want to make him or myself unhappy, so I pretended I didn't hear his concerned drawl. I curled into my window-seat, gazing out.

A moment had arrived. It wasn't something I'd set out for and had now reached, it had just come along like a taxi and picked me up. I was getting out of Hong Kong, and in spite of what I'd said to Clara, I didn't know if I wanted to return. A part of my life was over, it was over suddenly and a new life was going to unfold from here, after my year-long tarry in the Departure Lounge. *Afresh*. I whispered the word aloud, listened to the sound and liked it. It sounded like eating, like biting into an apple. There's a Larkin poem, less dismal than most, which ends *Afresh, afresh, afresh*. That would be me, I thought, marching forward into the future. Below me a tiny ship was pulling its turbulent wake across the sea. I closed my eyes. Tried to sleep.

Scarborough. Four midgets were living in a scaled-down house on the esplanade. Max and I looked in their small windows and watched them. I was five, Max was eight. We saw Father reading a small newspaper, Mother eating a small piece of toast, the children listening to small records. For weeks afterwards the house was in my dreams. I decided I was shrinking, checked myself against the door-jamb and convinced myself that the notches were getting lower. I carried this fear around with me, imagining bone-reduction, flesh-compaction, blood-evaporation. Dwindling of the tissue and ebbing of the fingernails.

Finally, I told Max. 'Max, I think I'm shrinking, I think I'm going to have to live in that little house, with those people.'

He didn't contradict me or sneer. He stood me back-to-back with him in front of a mirror, and showed me that he was still four inches taller than me, no more than before. And he said, 'Gloria, if you're shrinking, I'm shrinking too, and I'll go and live in the house with you.'

I opened my eyes, unsure if I'd been dreaming or consciously remembering. I'd been full of worries in those days, and Max was the one I turned to. I'd had no clear notion of the boundaries: what was fantasy, and what life might really do to you.

The aeroplane was making a constant yawning noise. I forgot it for a while and then noticed it again, and then thought I could detect a faint up-and-down lilt to it, like a police siren that had lost its voice. I wriggled, cramped and uncomfortable. Hours had passed and time was still slippery. I altered my watch. I was tired and fidgety, itchy too, and my bum and my back ached. Bumps seemed to be growing in my seat.

I stared out of the window at a village in a cleft of the mountains and wondered what it was like to live there. I stared at the back of the seat in front. Stretched my legs and waggled my toes and stared at them. The fat man beside me grunted, and his arm brushed my elbow. He lifted his head and his mild, offended eyes snagged mine. Then they closed again. I noticed a small food stain on his right leg, just above the knee; a speckle of, I guessed, mustard. This got me thinking about the meal he'd had before leaving, and whether he'd eaten alone. The whole long drag of his life lurked behind that vulnerable expression and that drip of mustard. And here was I, erecting this silent barrier between us, making it harder for him to pretend that he wasn't lonely. If I'd felt like talking I'd have told him it was my mother's fault. Stella never got the hang of small-talk, couldn't see the point of it. She could be scathing at the expense of other people. *What's in that woman's head? Shredded Wheat? It's a wonder she dares open her mouth.* It used to make us laugh.

I got up painfully, squeezed past him, and shuffled off to the loo for a piss and some stretching. All of me ached, except what chafed or itched. I bolted the door and in the confined grey space I undid everything, then locked my fingers and pulled, looking at my whitening knuckles in front of my nose. I let go of my fingers and pushed my elbows behind my shoulders. Did a few dips, knees pointing at opposite walls. Rolled my head around like an imbecile.

I sat on the loo and tried to evacuate the food and alcohol of the past several hours. I wanted to feel clean, scraped out and hollow, but it didn't work, it left me with a vague, heavy sense of unwellness, and I felt grubby and physically despondent as I zipped and buttoned myself back into my clothes. I returned to my seat reluctantly, as if it was a form of punishment, but I was just in time to see the ragged edge of England. I stared at the coast, imagining Max waiting in the Arrivals Lounge, with his half-smile, only one side of his mouth turned up, as if part of him was enjoying himself, part of him just watching.

The first thing I was going to have to do, was get used to him not being there. Not get over it, just get accustomed to his absence. At the moment it felt like a mistake, a misunderstanding that would soon be fixed. I remembered my head, at five years old, pressed neatly into the curve of his neck. Tears were squeezing out, but I ignored them. His funeral had happened a couple of hours ago. I'd intended to think about it, try to picture it, but I'd been asleep. It still felt like if I wanted Max to be alive enough then he'd be alive, smiling at me because I'd been silly enough to think he might have died. They'd announce it over the tannoy— *Would Ms Gloria Rumat go to the Information Desk where her brother is waiting for her.* He'd laugh at me; we'd both laugh.

I felt a hand on my arm. Gentle. I didn't turn round, but I didn't flinch or move either. I was holding the bridge of my nose as the tears streamed down my face, and I let the fat man's bare, consoling hand lie where it was, until the seat-belt light came on and we both sat up and word-lessly prepared to be in England.

I'd landed, found my luggage, been through customs, and hired a car. I'd sat in the car and pulled the seat forward. I'd smelt tobacco and some sour-fruit odour of polish. I'd speculated about the long-legged smoker who'd been here before me, what their journey had been, how it had gone for them. All this before I picked up the map, found the page with the airport and the big stain of Manchester on it, and abruptly wondered if I was doing the right thing.

I broke open my Duty Free carton, almost pulled the packet apart in getting a cigarette out, and lit up. I needed a few minutes. Everything had been happening too quickly. Everything was still happening too quickly. Why was I here? I'd come for the funeral, and now I'd missed it. What was left was duty: I was going to have to look through Max's things. There was this man to meet, Stephen. I took a long slow drag. Told myself I was in the right place. I was doing the right thing. *Afresh*. It was like the sound of cold water splashing into a basin.

Five minutes later. Just five minutes. The light was red and I was at the front of the queue, trying to read the map. A young red-haired man was walking along the verge. I thought he was going to wash my windscreen or try to sell me flowers. He saw me looking and nodded, like we were friends. I stared at the road, trying to keep track of him from the corner of my eye. Where was he? There was a blur of movement at the side-window, then the passenger door opened and he jabbed his head in.

'I need a favour.'

His voice was nasal. The syllables seemed to jab at me.

'Get lost.'

He got in the car. He pushed the map and the cigarettes off the passenger seat and sat down. He said, 'I need your help.' I said, 'Get out of the car.' The surge of fear I felt was indistinguishable from excitement. 'Go on.' I was shouting now. 'Get out!'

He nearly did. I saw his eyes flick towards the door. He probably only stayed where he was because it was too embarrassing to give up so easily.

He said, 'No, listen, just a favour, right? That's all.' The woman behind me hooted her horn. 'Better move,' he said.

I drove through the lights, and across the junction, then pulled over. Was he planning to rape me? My thighs squeezed together, my breaths were fast and shallow. I had a hand on the door, ready to jump out and run into the road.

'No,' I said. 'I can't help you.'

I could see the self-belief draining out of him. 'I'm just hitching,' he was a bit plaintive now. 'No one's stopped, and I'm desperate.'

Welcome to England. I'd only been away for a year. Is this what it was like now? I found I'd become calm—life's boundaries are never as fixed as we think. Ambushes and surprises are always possible. Sudden shrinkings, sudden moves to Hong Kong, sudden deaths. And I felt better for having shouted at him, like I'd been carrying that anger around with me.

'Right,' he said, 'here, take my mobile.' He took it out and handed it to me.

'What's this for?'

'Keep it till you drop me. You want something else? You can have my wallet, seriously, but it's empty.'

I stared at him. 'Why are you doing this?'

'I need cash. Not from you, from a mate in Birmingham.' He nodded at the sign for the motorway.

I almost laughed. 'I'm not going to Birmingham.'

'But you could. Whatever you're doing, it could wait, right? I'm definitely not going to hurt you. All I want is a lift, and you'll save my life.'

Now that I looked more carefully, I wasn't sure he could hurt me. He was pale and underfed. He had hot red hair and a few splotchy freckles. He wore an ugly anorak. He looked back at me. His eyes were hazel. They were curious and direct and didn't seem to be hiding anything.

Whatever you're doing, it could wait. I didn't answer, but I pulled out of the lay-by and headed for the motorway.

'Sweet,' he said. 'I'm Robbie, what's your name?'

'Gloria.' I accelerated down the slip road, wondering what I was doing. I no longer felt threatened, but still wished I was wearing jeans and an old sweater, rather than a skirt and a shirt. I'd have felt happier wrapped in heavy denim and a belt. 'So you're not going to try to rape me?'

'No.' He stretched the syllable, indignant. 'What do you think I am?'

'Sorry,' I said, 'am I offending you? It's just, you jumped in my car and scared the shit out of me.'

'You didn't look scared.' he said. Now he was grinning at me, like we were mates. 'You were cool.'

We drove quietly for a while. I played the number-plate game, making headlines. *Bald Vicar Executed. King To Abdicate.* Concentrating on that, feeling pleased I hadn't looked scared.

'So,' he said, 'where you from, Gloria?'

This, I sensed, was Robbie trying to put me at my ease.

'Hong Kong,' I said. 'I've been there for a year.'

'I see, I see, and now you're back?'

'My brother died.'

'I see, I see, I'm sorry.'

He sounded genuinely apologetic, a touch nervous. Some men, even grown men, married men, are like that when they talk to women. It seems to be a lifetime affliction for them.

'My brother died,' I repeated, looking for sympathy, even remorse. 'And I've missed his funeral. This is in fact just the last thing I need.'

He was nodding at me, a small, fast movement, sympathetic, as if it was a shame but there was nothing he could do to help. He unzipped his anorak a little, revealing a T-shirt with an Adidas logo.

'Someone's expecting me,' I said. 'My brother's friend. When I don't show up he might call the police.'

'Use the mobile,' said Robbie. I didn't answer. 'Anyway, he'll think you've gone to your mum's or something.'

'My mother's dead too.'

'Dad?'

'All dead.'

He made a noise, like *Whew*. 'That's tough,' he said.

There was a pause. Someone at school had told me mirrors were doors angels could come and go through. It was meant to make me feel better when my father died. It didn't. It made me uneasy. At night I hung a pillowcase over my mirror to close the door. Because who'd want an angel creeping into her bedroom, in his cotton nightdress, with his silly smile and his big clumsy wings? Who'd want an angel if she had a kind older brother?

I had an image suddenly of Max sitting on my bed, swapping memories of Dad with me. I tried to hold the picture, but Robbie wanted to keep the conversation stumbling along.

'So, what'd he die of? Your dad.'

'Old age,' I said, to shut him up. In fact, as far as I could tell, time killed him. It transformed him when I wasn't looking, made him elderly, and fragile, loose-skinned and brittle-boned. It messed with his character too, so he seemed puzzled by life, increasingly out of step with the flow of it. Time killed him with its hard magic, but my mother helped. They wore him down together, they wore him out.

'OK, suppose this,' said Robbie. 'Suppose someone said they'd break your legs if they found you, you'd want to be somewhere else, right?'

'I'd tell the police.'

'Suppose you couldn't do that.'

'This is your situation? What, you owe money?'

'See, I don't want to make your life difficult.'

'Too late.'

'There's a guy in Birmingham will give me money. If I'm back with it tonight, I'm OK. You're the good Samaritan here. What I'm actually doing here, right, is making you feel good about yourself.'

'Big of you.'

'Seriously, this is life or death and you're saving my life, and all it takes is a ride to Birmingham.'

More silence. *Young Traveller Expires*. I was sure there was a flaw in his thinking, but I couldn't immediately spot it. Still, I felt more comfortable in my skin now, and in my clothes. But conversation would be too much of a concession. I took deep breaths. It seemed he didn't need much prompting to talk. In other circumstances I might have asked him for some tips on how to meet people. If I was more like Robbie, I'd have told my whole story to the man on the plane. I'd feel more comfortable about meeting Stephen.

'See, I buy this new guitar, because we've got this gig and we're about to get signed, and they say: "Love the band, love the sound, lose Robbie." And I'm like: "We come as a unit, take it or leave it," but the others are all like: "OK, Robbie's out." You believe that? So I've got no band, no friends, and a big debt, from buying the guitar.'

A pause.

'You think you've got mates,' he said. 'Turns out you've got nothing.'

He seemed to notice that I wasn't talking.

'Gloria, come on, you're not still pissed off?'

'Mostly with myself,' I said. 'You talk a lot, don't you?'

'Oh, yeah.' He seemed to think it was a compliment. 'Can't stop.' He was quiet for about a second, and then: 'Seriously though, sorry about your brother. What happened?'

First I didn't answer, and then, after a moment, I did. 'The truth is,' I told him, slowly, as if I was talking to myself, 'he wasn't the best brother.'

I heard this like he did, as if it was brand new. I wondered if it was true, and why I was telling him. He was unsurprised.

'I don't get on with mine either. He's a wanker.'

'Max wasn't a wanker, he just wasn't a great brother.' I wanted to say he was marvellous, and when he died the shine went out of everything, but it would have been a lie. He was good at holding my hand when I was a girl, and good later at turning up and getting attention, and being generous and funny in short bursts. He was not good at staying, and spending time. 'I always hoped we'd get closer as we got older.'

'How'd he die?'

Maybe Clara had been too sensitive, too scared of hurting me, but she must have been thinking the same way I was.

'He killed himself,' I said.

Arrival

I hope you're not kidding yourself that Max
fell under that train?
Come on, one thing we know about Max,
he wasn't clumsy.
Get used to it, he killed himself.
And I know why.
You know too.

The second anonymous letter was scrunched in Stephen's pocket. Whoever it was, had chosen to send it on the morning of Max's funeral. He was going to have to think about it soon, but not yet, not yet. He needed, he felt, recovery time.

Friday afternoon. He and Katie lay there like they'd been dropped from the ceiling, Stephen on the floor and Katie all along the sofa, coshed by exhaustion. They'd spent Thursday night talking and drinking, dozing occasionally, then talking some more, never quite making it up to bedrooms. How this was the first death in their lives. How they were getting to an age though, when they worried about their parents' health. How it was an accident (Stephen). How if it wasn't, no one was to blame, and guilt anyway was a useless emotion (Katie). They talked and were silent, talked some more. As if they were spending all night trying to define something, trying to reach a conclusion and failing, piling up words but always

27

failing. How grief felt not too great but too unwieldy to contain, as if it was an awkward, ill-defined shape that would not fit into the ordinary contours of their lives.

Then Gloria's non-appearance, calls to the airport, and the funeral happening in an odd, almost illicit way, without her. Already Stephen's memory of the event seemed compressed and unreliable, something he'd watched on television rather than something that had actually happened. He'd contacted friends, and found an aunt in Max's address book. He'd guessed Max would have wanted a Humanist ceremony. He'd contacted them and let them take over. A kind woman in a dark suit led the service, her tone gentle, almost coaxing, as if one of the mourners had said something unreasonable to her, and she was arguing them round. He'd noticed her *Star Trek*-style split infinitive, *to peacefully go*. 'Peacefully' was hardly appropriate. Then it was over and Katie had come back to the house with him, to make sure he was all right, apparently.

Stephen looked blearily at his watch. 'You have to go,' he said. 'She's meant to be here, Gloria, she's meant to be here already.'

Katie lifted her feet from the sofa and pointed her toes at the ceiling.

'Are you going to cope?' she said.

Stephen shrugged.

'Don't.' She sat up. 'Don't go all quiet.' Leaning forward, as if she had important news to impart. 'I've seen you like this before, after what happened with Jude.'

He said nothing.

'Make me something to eat,' said Katie, 'then I'll go.'

They ate bacon sandwiches at the small table in the kitchen. Katie wondered about dropping in on her new man. Would he be pleased to see her, or would he think just showing up was a bit needy? Stephen offered no opinion. He avoided her eyes, wished she'd hurry up and leave. She was a good friend, but he'd never spent quite so long in her company before. She got on his nerves sometimes, tended to nag him about feelings. Women think they're experts on feelings, but it doesn't stop them messing up their lives. In Stephen's opinion, Katie didn't have lovers, she had symptoms. You heard who she was sleeping with, or met them, and you thought What is *wrong* with her?

She left, after some ushering, after he'd promised to call and tell her about Gloria, and promised to arrange a meeting. He stood in the doorway and watched her go, scanning the street for potential Glorias on her way.

He closed the door before she was out of sight, and let his back slide down it until he was sitting on the mat. Lowered his head on to his raised knees and laced his fingers into his hair. Everyone had said it had gone well, they'd asked if he'd be all right, there'd been pats and hugs. *Yes, yes*, he'd said, *thanks, fine*. Most of them, like him, weren't used to bereavement. Stephen found it made his body feel unfamiliar. He was aware that sliding down the door smacked of melodrama, but it felt the most appropriate thing because he didn't want to have to move his body or hold it upright. Running might have been an option, shaking himself like a towel might have been an option, but he felt a bit too soggy for that, so he just slumped instead on the stiff bristles of the mat, balled up like a child trying to make himself small.

I gave Robbie his mobile. He smiled sheepishly.

'Sorry,' he said, 'I was desperate. But you were sound, better than I deserve.'

Not true. He'd scared me briefly and then intrigued

me, but the real reason I hadn't ordered him out of the car was nothing to do with my good nature; it was because I was happy to put off meeting Stephen.

'Seriously, you've honestly saved my life. Let me give you this.'

He started scribbling something on a scrap of paper. I glanced at it, my eyes moving from the road to his lap. He offered it, and when I didn't move to take it, he squashed it into my hand.

'Get in touch, I'll pay you for your petrol, whatever. I owe you one.'

I dropped him on a roundabout on the A38, went all the way around it and headed back up the motorway. His scrap of paper was still balled into my fist. Shoving it into my pocket, I found a card. *Greg Davidson, IT Consultant.* The fat man on the plane had introduced himself as Greg, before he'd realised I wasn't feeling talkative. He must have slipped his card into my pocket. Greg and Robbie. It seemed I knew people in England after all. A fat, mustard-stained computer geek, and a garrulous failed band-member. And next, Stephen. I should be keen to meet him, keen to discover what he could tell me about Max's life, and death, but he felt like an irrelevance as I raced towards him, a social challenge standing between me and my brother, no more promising than Greg or Robbie.

The phone was ringing. Stephen lifted his head off his knees and looked at his watch, puzzled. Still no Gloria? He unfolded himself painfully and hobbled down the hall.

'Hello?'

'Steve? Hi, Tim Griffin here, Griffin Agency.'

'Yeah, hi.' Stephen's brain was only slowly meshing into gear.

'Heavy night?

'Sorry?'

'You sound a bit spaced. Your script, remember? I'm calling about your script.'

'Sorry, yes, I remember.'

'Liked it, very promising. I think we should talk.'

Stephen stuttered and stalled as he slowly registered what was being said.

'Yes, yes,' he said. 'We should talk.'

He said the right things, arranged a meeting on Tuesday.

'All right, see you then. Bye.'

Stephen put the phone down. There was too much going on for him to hold in his head. He went slowly upstairs and wrote down the date of his meeting with Griffin. He wondered if he should call the airport again. Or perhaps the AA, to find out about accidents. Instead, he turned on his laptop. *Liked it, very promising, I think we should talk.*

They are in Simon's classroom. a pause before he speaks.

SIMON: If you were going to insult me . . .

ROSE: Yes?

SIMON: What would you say?

ROSE: This is dangerous.

SIMON: I'm interested.

ROSE: Why?

SIMON: We shouldn't have secrets.

ROSE: Yes, we should. I like my secrets, they give me texture.

SIMON: I'd call you self-obsessed.

ROSE: What?

SIMON: If I was going to insult you.

ROSE: You're a narcissist, this whole idea is narcissistic. You're also inward and uptight.

SIMON: See, you're getting the hang of it.

ROSE: I don't like the way you wash-up, or the way you eat.

SIMON: OK.

ROSE: You're too tidy, and I don't like your friends.

SIMON: Even Mike?

ROSE: Mike's an arsehole.

SIMON: *(protesting)* Rose.

ROSE: What do you mean I'm self-obsessed? Justify that.

SIMON: Move in with me.

ROSE: Pardon?

On Rose, surprised, considering.

He began an email to a friend, about Max. His fingers were draped over the keyboard when he saw Gloria. He was halfway through the email. *We're shocked*, he'd written, then deleted it. *We can't believe it.* He'd often pause and look out of the window when marking or planning a lesson. His terrace was on the side of the valley and he'd stare at the hillside opposite, or the tall houses of Hebden Bridge jostling below. He'd watch young mothers bent behind pushchairs, walking slowly up the steep road outside. Something he liked about the sight, something focused. The purpose in the heavy step, the forward lean of the spine, a sense of a shaped life.

He stopped writing, rocked back in his chair, looked out of the window and saw Gloria.

He assumed it was her. She was dressed in black, but trendy black, not funeral black. A denim jacket and a skirt and a shirt which showed the solid shape of her. Shoulders and hips. Blonde. As he watched she got out of her car, got her case out of the boot, and then yelled at a man who was passing.

It was odd, she got her case out in no hurry, locked the boot, straightened, and then started shouting. Maybe a look was exchanged, or some words. The man replied, Stephen could see he was shouting too, but she was round the car and in his face immediately, and he thought *There's going to be a fight*, he wondered if he should run down and intervene. The man backed off. He literally backed away a few paces, like he didn't want to take his eyes off her, then he turned and walked quickly down the hill as Gloria shouted something after him.

She stood and watched him for a few seconds. Then she set herself, there was a movement of her shoulders and her head, and she crossed the road and came towards the house.

Stephen stood up, stepped away from the window and tried to fix his face, so it wouldn't be obvious he'd seen what he'd just seen. He looked in the mirror on the landing and practised an expression. Neutral and serious, with a hint of friendliness. It reminded him of the woman who'd led the Humanist service. That was something to aim for, her composure. He pushed a hand through his hair and waited for the bell to ring. It didn't. He waited some more, then hurried down the stairs, puzzled. Perhaps she'd lost the number of the house? But he could see her dark shape through the frosted glass. She was waiting. She finally rang the bell as he opened the door.

'I saw you in the window,' she said. 'Saw you get up, thought you'd seen me.'

'No, sorry. I'm Stephen, hello.' He was going for confident but sombre. Panting a little and transparently lying with his first word to her.

'Hello.' She looked at him.

'We're all very, we're very . . .'

'I know. So am I.'

She stood there on the doorstep and he faced her as if deliberately barring her way. Both nodding, only managing glancing eye-contact. There was an unsettled, breathless sense about her too. He'd have taken it for grief if he hadn't just seen her yelling.

He stepped aside and Gloria walked in.

In the kitchen she fell into a chair, put her hands over the lower half of her face and said 'Tea?' through her fingers.

Her clothes were creased and her face was puffy. Her hands hid her expression, and her eyes were sleepy. She looked at him suddenly, catching him studying her. He smiled weakly, wanting to hug her, or come up with some words to reassure and welcome her, but this was where the size of what had happened and the odd shape of grief got in the way. Instead, he asked about the flight and she said a few words. She said she was sad she'd missed the funeral, and he shook his head.

'No,' he said, 'it was nothing.'

What on earth did he mean by that? It sounded like he was either accepting her apology for not being there, or telling her the funeral and her absence were of no consequence. She gave him a quizzical look, but let it go. What could he say? He didn't want to talk yet about how close he'd been to Max, about how Max had seemed in the weeks running up to his death, about whether he had killed himself. So instead he told her how he'd heard the news. Ordinary, incontrovertible facts. Perhaps there was something reassuring in the way that strangers had carried this information to him and calmly delivered it.

He'd answered the door to the police. A man and a woman, in black and white.

The woman spoke. 'Does a Max Rumat live here?' There was a collection of hints in her face and in her tone, in the tilt of her head, in the way the man with her looked curiously at his feet.

'Yes,' he said. 'Pronounced *Rumour*. French grandfather.'

They'd found the address in his wallet. They were going carefully in case Stephen was a family member, or perhaps Max's lover, but when they found he was just a friend, sharing the house, he saw them relax. A slight lowering of the shoulders and a shift in their faces. They wanted addresses for Max's next of kin, which meant Gloria and the aunt, and then they wanted some idea of how his mood had been lately. Stephen was staring at a dust shadow on the man's dark shoulder. At least they were never going to look inappropriately cheerful on errands like these.

'So, can you tell me anything about his mood?'

It seemed a difficult question.

'You know,' said the policeman. 'Was he down? Was he depressed?'

'He's always depressed,' Stephen said, with an edge of impatience, as if everyone should know this.

The policewoman stared at him. The wrong tense hovered in the air and Stephen had to resist an urge to correct it. He felt he should say something else, something to define his friendship with Max. He wanted their stilted formality back, he wanted the policewoman to look concerned and offer him a cup of tea. No words came.

Gloria sipped her tea and listened politely. She listened to the story of the police then put down her cup.

'I think I'm going to puke,' she said.

Stephen pointed her towards the bathroom and stood back. She ran up the stairs and soon he heard her hoarse retching as if someone was torturing her in there. He didn't know what to do. He washed up the tea things, feeling tearful but holding it back for her sake. He had noticed that this happened. Tears crept up on him not when he was thinking about Max, but when he was doing something banal which loosened the jigsaw of his thoughts, leaving a space for grief to creep in.

When she came back, she apologised, said something about too much travelling, said she'd never been so tired. Stephen took her to Max's room and then left her alone. He went to his room, tired too. So far, he'd found her difficult. He'd felt sad for her, but he'd found her difficult. She had a greater claim on Max than he did, she had a right to consider herself more bereaved. And there was an awkwardness in this stranger coming here to take away his friend's possessions. And he'd had a feeling, because of sideways glances, because of a certain stillness about her, that he was being weighed. Assessed. And there was a slight but distinct smell about her.

He left her and retreated back to his bedroom.

She was on the other side of the thin wall. He could hear himself telling Katie. *She was in tatters. She threw up.* Katie would say *Poor girl, I hope you were nice to her?* She'd probably have an image of him with an arm round Gloria's shoulders as she bent over the toilet. He looked at his neatly shelved books and CDs, the sound system not much bigger than a hardback, the blocky red Matisse print on the white walls. He seemed to be seeing it all through Gloria's eyes. He imagined she'd be critical and he thought about how he'd respond. He heard movement. Something dropped and there was a short sound, pain or anger. She'd be fingering Max's things, she'd be picking them up and putting them down, she'd be prowling, as if someone had locked her up in there and she was

searching for a way out. There was a stranger in his house.
It was as if grief finally had a shape.

Saturday

The Max Museum

STEPHEN THOUGHT HE could hear her stirring. He sat up, drew the curtain so he could see sky and tree-tops, then lay back under the duvet, half-listening, thinking about what to tell her. He'd begin with how he met Max.

He'd been in The Shoulder of Mutton, waiting for Jude. She was twenty minutes late when she rang his mobile and told him she couldn't make it. He ordered another pint. He'd been planning to point out the tall man to her, in the check shirt and the tan jacket, the Sainsbury's bag at his feet with something lumpy inside it, that bit of fur sticking out of the top. He paid for his pint, took a drink. Maybe he should end it with Jude. Maybe he should call her back and say *Guess what, it's over.*

He approached the tall man and said, 'I've been trying to work out what's in your bag.' It came out sounding like they were halfway through an argument, his anger towards Jude spilling over. He hoped he wasn't about to get into a fight. The man looked well-built, and even sitting down he had a settled, physical confidence about him.

But Max smiled. Stephen had read how to spot a genuine smile: it fades slowly. Max looked up at him with a pleased, slow-fading smile and said, 'Guess.'

Stephen sat down and guessed at a hat, a pair of gloves, a child's toy. Max shook his head. Stephen tried a camera, some smoke, a small tree. Max suggested he feel the bag. Beneath the plastic, Stephen felt a thin layer of soft material over a brittle, ridged shape.

'I've been stood up,' he said, as he fingered the object.

Max moved his head. 'It happens.'

'Is this an animal?'

That smile again. 'Used to be.'

It was his landlord's cat, a tortoiseshell with, once, a croaky miaow. The previous night it had the cat-shivers, and this morning it was dead, stiff and dead. Max had snapped its tail. It was sticking out of the bag like a string without a balloon, so he snapped it.

They left together, went down the alley towards the station and met three men heading unsteadily the other way, singing. Stephen saw what was coming, wanted to turn back, but it was too late. One of the men shoved him against the wall and put his arm in his throat, the other two grabbed Max. They had a bit of loose change and one credit card between them, neither was even wearing a watch.

'Take the bag,' said Max, 'take it.' They took their prize, a dead, snapped cat, and ran. Stephen massaged his throat, coughed and looked at his new friend. Max continued their earlier conversation as if they hadn't been interrupted.

'If you love her,' he said, 'of course you can't end it. As long as you're prepared to get hurt.'

No sign of Gloria downstairs, she was having a late start. Stephen picked up the post, separated the third letter from the rest, took it to the kitchen table, feeling queasy. What would Max have done in this situation?

So you've met Gloria.

What do you make of her?
Is she like Max,
(except a better person in every way)?
What do you think?
Are you likely to sleep with her?
Given that you're a disaster with women,
what do you think?

'Fuck off.' He said it out loud. 'Fuck off.' Three letters in three days. Stephen wanted to meet this person and tell them *This mad letter thing, it's not original, it's not big or clever.* He laid all three out on the kitchen table and stared at them. Felt the paper, smelt it, examined the typeface. He looked round quickly when he thought he heard a noise from upstairs. He wasn't sure he wanted Gloria to see them. Nothing. It was his imagination. He read them all again.

This was a story. Stephen thought he could discern in stories the secret histories of individuals. There was a bread knife on the kitchen table. He felt stories helped him to see the inner geography of other people's lives. He picked up the knife and stabbed the third letter with it, then scored the page with the blade's serrated edge. Right now, he didn't care about stories. If the letter-writer had been in the room with him, he might have used the knife on them. He had a suspicion he knew who it was. He thought it was Jude.

At 11 a.m. he knocked on Gloria's door, opened it a crack and put his head round. She was raised up on an elbow and had a sick bowl beside her. There was a sweet-shop smell in the room, like over-ripe fruit.

'So,' he tried. 'Are you er . . . Are you all right?'

She lifted her eyes and looked at him as if she was wondering who he was.

❧

Greg Davidson and the man with the urn had been sitting next to each other on the tulip seats, heads bent together, whispering. *She's not all there, that one.* I walked away, dignified, but on the next row of seats a couple were having sex. It was Clara and a man I didn't recognise. He turned his head and grinned up at me, hips still pumping. I laid a road map over his bare arse, then searched all around the Departure Lounge, expecting to see Max.

That was 04:12 according to the green digits of his clock radio. Dark outside, so it was in the morning. I got out of bed and slipped, naked, to the loo. Pissed in the dark and didn't flush. On the landing I hesitated, not sure which door I'd come out of. Naked in the middle of the night in a stranger's house. I crept to the first door, and heard Stephen's breathing. Went back to Max's room, found one of his shirts and put it on. Then I got back into bed.

When I woke up I was feeling ill again. Awake, and fairly alert, I was wishing I hadn't missed the funeral. I wanted to have seen his coffin being lowered into the ground, wanted an authoritative vicar to say something resonant. Perhaps there would have been some sort of viewing beforehand. I tried to imagine Max's face, still and colourless, looking too thin or too plump depending on what the undertaker had done with it, but still recognisably him, still with some sense that my brother had recently been there.

I wished I hadn't missed the funeral, and I wished I'd never gone to Hong Kong, had stuck with the arts admin job instead, or applied for the place on the journalism course. There are many things I'd change, if I could. I'd lose my virginity with Graham Cracknell instead of Peter

Steel, and I'd do the Spanish A level instead of Politics, and I wouldn't go to that Del Amitri gig when we had a car crash on the way home and I broke my wrist. I'd never have slept with Mike Harper, and Jenny Campion wouldn't have spilled red wine on my cream linen dress five minutes after I got to her party. I'd spend more time with Max, and phone him if I didn't see him. I'd find amusing things to tell him. He'd say, *Gloria always knows how to switch on my lights*.

There was foul tasting saliva in my mouth. I spat it into the bowl. You accept things like Peter Steel, Mike Harper and Jenny Campion, you work around them, because life isn't perfect. Max dying was different. I didn't know if I could work around that. I wished Stephen was dead and Max alive. I wanted me to have come back to console Max over the death of his friend. I'd hug him, he'd say, *I'm so glad you're here for me*. It would be something to bond over, a new start for us both. How would Stephen have died? He wouldn't have the guts to kill himself—he'd fall down some steps and break his neck. He was not what I'd wanted to meet. Max's good friend. I'd been hoping for someone more like Max.

This was the thought in my head when he barged in and probably got a flash of my tits as I retched. When he'd gone, I sat up and began for the first time to register Max's bedroom. Big windows, plenty of light. A narrow bed and a firm mattress. Three pillows, none of them with a head-shaped dent or any trace of a human smell. I'd checked, snuffled at them, searching for his scent.

Thirsty, my stomach empty and my mouth sour, I went to the bathroom, started a bath running, then went back in the bedroom. Max's slim laptop was on his desk. I sat down, opened it, pressed the Power button and clicked on to his email.

Clara hi it's me. I'm in Hebden Bridge and I don't like it. Too many trees all pimply like broccoli. Don't like Stephen either. He comes in this morning right and I'm lying there like a rag, some stomach thing from airline food, and half-naked, and he just marches in and asks am I ok like he expects me to get up and shake his hand. And I'm not even going to tell you about being kidnapped that can wait. Missed the funeral though. Can't believe I missed it but I did. And now I'm wondering why I'm here. I picture Stephen having lunch alone. Boiled eggs in the kitchen with radio for company. Listening to the News same as it was an hour ago. I don't like the house—too tidy. Got to go bath's running. Still no plans for the future. You can contact me here. Love, G.

A wooden box filigreed in silver stood next to the laptop. I picked it up and held it against my cheek. It was lighter than I'd expected, hollow, and the cool metal pressed its pattern into my skin. I wanted something of mine in his room, so I found my purse, unzipped it, and took out the hermit crab's shell from where it lived among the mixed Chinese and English coins. Held it for a moment between finger and thumb, twisting it. A memento. Something I'd picked up on the beach on the last day I'd spent with Max. I placed it on the bedside table.

Half-sunk and still sleepy, I lifted water in the bent palm of my hand and poured it slowly over my stomach. I'd been in Max's bed, and his shirt, and now I was in his bath, filling the spaces he'd filled hundreds of times in the past. His ghost was in the house. I felt the outline of him, was aware of him just beyond the corner of my eye, as if he'd only just left and there was still a Max-shaped disturbance in the air.

I ran cold water and splashed my face with it. Washed

quickly and thoroughly. Waking up, waking up. Time to have another go at meeting Stephen.

It was hard to know what to do with my feelings. You can't grieve all day, you can't eat breakfast in a grief-stricken fashion. The kitchen was colourful. There was a lot of red formica, a bright bulb in a paper shade, a bright print on the wall. I picked up a section of yesterday's paper, put it down again. Next to it, a mug of half-drunk coffee, three typed envelopes, a bread knife and a saucer of earth.

I could hear Stephen in the loo, so I quickly took the first letter out of its envelope and read it. It seemed to me that reading something private would be a good way to get to know him. The toilet flushed. I put the first one back and took out the second. This was more interesting than I'd anticipated. Read the second, replaced it and took out the third. It nearly fell to pieces in my hand. Someone had stabbed the word *Gloria*. Jesus. *Are you likely to sleep with her?* I could hear him washing his hands. He'd be out in a minute. I looked at the bread knife. Would he stab me if he found me with his letters? I shoved the last one back in its envelope as he entered, and picked up a corner of the paper, pretending something there had caught my attention, Stephen entering in the same hurried moment. Had he seen me replacing the last letter? He seemed to pause, then spoke.

'How are you?'

'Yes, I'm fine.'

I saw him better this morning. A skinny, pale teacher with dark rings round his eyes, as if it was him who'd just got off the long-haul flight. Short brown hair, sticking up in places. I could imagine him at the basin, washing his hands then pushing his wet fingers over his scalp. He wore a blue shirt with the sleeves rolled up. His voice was kind, but there was a wary edge to his look, as if he thought I might suddenly throw up again, or start crying. Or as if he'd seen me reading his unusual post.

He said, 'I keep expecting him to walk through the door.'

There was a loaf on the breadboard, so I took a piece of granary out of the bag, and put it in the toaster.

'I feel like we should know each other better,' Stephen continued, 'given that we both knew Max so well.'

I gave a small nod, barely acknowledging his words, not looking at him. Then there was a silence so I did look at him and saw that he was offended. This was why I'd been reluctant to meet him, this was exactly what I didn't want: the awkward challenge of getting to know someone, the special difficulty of the subject of Max waiting to be teased and probed and discussed. I'm not good with strangers. I'm not much good with conversation in general. My mother told me breath was too precious to be wasted on words. That doesn't prepare you for a moment like this. Hoping to mollify, I tried an easy line I often use with men.

'Tell me about yourself.'

He paused. 'I'm a teacher.' Keeping it short.

'Like it?'

I knew as soon as the words were out of my mouth what he was going to do. He gave a small nod, like the subject didn't interest him. Tit for tat. The two of us were stumbling like party guests hoping someone more interesting was going to turn up. We were going to have to try harder—the more interesting person definitely wasn't coming.

I thought I could smell burning.

'And I collect things,' Stephen said.

'What do you collect?' A sigh in my voice. The sad

habits of men. Men with their cars and gadgets and their lists of statistics, which are all about ordering the world into something tame and dull.

Something was definitely burning.

Stephen said, 'Stories, for instance.'

This sounded affected, but I didn't respond because as he spoke flames spat out of the toaster. We both panicked.

I tried to sound calm. 'You're not meant to put water on electrics, are you?'

'I don't know. Switch it off.'

I pulled it away from the wall and unplugged it, then tried to stifle it with a tea towel. The tea towel caught fire.

'Sink!' Stephen shouted.

But I dropped the tea towel, unfortunately on to another section of newspaper which also caught fire. Odd how with just a little stupidity a moment can slip from clumsy or comic towards danger. I jumped on the burning newspaper, stamping on it, dancing. Stephen dropped the toaster in the sink and threw the saucer of earth on to the newspaper. Then for an odd moment, he was still shouting and I was still dancing even though there were no more flames.

We both took a few breaths.

He was smiling, but it was strained. 'This house was quite sane till you arrived.'

'Don't worry,' I said, 'I'm not staying. What was that earth doing there?'

'From Max's grave.'

I looked down at the mess on the floor, moved it with my foot. 'Think you better get some more.' I laughed a little, and so did he. I could hear relief in it and I realised he was finding this meeting as awkward as I was.

'I'm sorry,' I said. 'I know I can be difficult.'

'No.' He stretched out his hand towards me, as if he

intended us to shake hands, but he just laid his fingers lightly on my arm. 'No.'

I nodded, then filled a glass of cold water and swallowed it all. I felt slightly off-balance, but Stephen's tentative touch seemed like a place for us to begin. I put the kettle on, gingerly, as he gathered burnt paper and earth into a bin bag. I noticed he took the opportunity to slide the letters into his pocket.

'You collect stories,' I prompted.

'Family stories, friends' stories,' he said.

I buttered some bread, nodding like I knew what he was talking about. Side-on to him, looking down at the breadboard. I was aware of his glance sliding up and down me, a quick eye-sweep, checking me out. Black T-shirt, pale cotton trousers. The kitchen smelt singed.

'Tell me one of Max's stories,' I said.

'Max claimed he didn't have any.'

I turned, and his eyes had moved back up to my face. 'Sounds like him.'

'But I can tell you how we met.'

We moved into the sitting room. Creamy walls, blue furniture and sunlight. I settled into the sofa by the window, looking at the hillside bulging on the other side of the valley, balancing my plate on my knees.

'There's more green in that window,' I said, 'than I saw in a year in Hong Kong.'

It wasn't true; as I spoke I had a vision of walking round Victoria Peak, where views of the city and the harbour gave way to a rocky green hillside similar to the one I saw here. But it was something to say. I wanted to leach the awkwardness out of this situation. So I sat opposite him with my bread and coffee, waiting, understanding that he'd thought about this, about mentioning the stories, about telling me how he met Max.

A pub, a dead cat, a mugging.

'They take the bag and run, and they end up with nothing but a snapped cat. Max and me end up friends.'

I was watching Stephen, more interested in him than his words. His emphasis was practised, his gestures seemed fluent, he looked like a teacher addressing a group. It was a safe, rehearsed way of making himself heard. I understood. Sometimes before a phone call I would work through almost an entire script before dialling the number. Then if the wrong person answered, I might put the phone down.

I nodded. 'It's good to hear about Max.'

This took us into unrehearsed territory. Stephen's eyes focused and he stared at me. I felt like he was looking for Max's face in mine. He asked, 'Were you close?'

The coffee was instant and by now almost cold, but I sipped it anyway, giving myself time. Were we close? We emailed occasionally. I told him everything was fine, told him I felt I was drifting a bit, but it felt OK. He told me he admired the way I'd gone out there, turned my life upside down. Said he was drifting too, so maybe it was a family trait. Like a cleft palate, he said, or webbed fingers.

I was aware that the silence was stretching. 'I'm his sister,' I said. 'Of course we were.' The two tenses seemed to clash inconsistently. I tried again. 'You said he was always depressed?'

'He'd be in bed all day complaining about his teeth, or his scalp, or his skin. There'd always be these small, physical problems. I'd say come for a drink, but he'd say no, not today, it's a bad day.' I looked at him, and he repeated it as if it might be unclear. 'He had these bad days.'

This was making me angry. Angry I hadn't known, and angry Stephen hadn't done something about it. 'And how about you? Were you close?'

'Yes,' said Stephen. 'We were.'

Shame you didn't help him then. I managed not to say this, but in the tense silence that followed it felt as if the words had been spoken. It was like we were drawing up battle lines. I took a slow breath, looked at my nails, then at Stephen.

'Let's go and have a look at Max's bedroom. Maybe you could explain a couple of things.'

I bolted my bread. We should have sat in the creamy sunlit room for a while longer and got to know each other, but the conversation wasn't going as well as either of us had hoped.

After the long night I'd spent in it, the bedroom had an unaired smell, like damp wool. My suitcase gaped, a bra on top looking grey-blue and tired. I tipped the lid shut with my foot and pushed the window open. Stood still a moment, feeling the air move around my face. When I turned, I picked up the bayonet lying on Max's desk.

'This is what I'm talking about,' I said. 'For a start. How do you explain this?'

Stephen sighed. He told me that Max was always finding things, getting excited about them. He'd plan to use them in some new piece, and then not get round to it. He'd found the bayonet in a skip a few weeks ago and got attached to it, carried it with him constantly, slept with it by his pillow.

Stephen became knowledgeable. This was Max's head, also on his desk, modelled in clay, roughly, so that you could see where his thumbs had pushed it into shape. It wasn't very like him, but the sharp nose was familiar, the straight line of the mouth. This was his sketch-pad, this was his favourite coat. Just a thin, tan bomber, nothing special. Stephen was like the curator of a small Max museum.

He came to my hermit crab's shell. 'Don't remember this.'

'It's mine.'

His hand stopped on the way to picking it up. It was the size of a thumbnail, the colour of wet paper, with a smooth-lipped hole curling round on itself. He raised an eyebrow, but I pretended not to notice. I opened a drawer in the desk, moved aside pencils, a ruler, a stapler, and pulled out a thick sheet of paper. 'And this?' I said. 'Who's this?'

It was a pencil sketch of a young woman. She might have been pretty, but Max had done something to her face, caricatured her teeth and hair, made her ugly.

Stephen was gratifyingly surprised. 'Rachel,' he said. 'I didn't know he'd done this.'

'He have something against her?'

'They barely met, and they didn't get on.'

He turned away. Sensitive subject, apparently.

He picked up the filigreed, hollow box. I watched it jealously, as if Stephen was about to slip it into his pocket. Max had taken some time over it. There were no nails involved, it was tongue and groove, a pale wood, perhaps maple, crafted, firmly fixed and polished, before he wound delicate strands of silver around it in an intricate pattern. I could see him planing a shaving off a thin wooden panel, the sweet-smelling curl rising like a beckoning finger. I could see him lowering his face to the raw surface, smelling it. It smelt of pear drops. Stephen held it nervously. We were both aware that there was something, possibly, hidden inside.

'Don't know how you feel about this,' Stephen scratched his face, his palm over his mouth, 'but I was hoping to keep it. Last thing he made, that I know of. As a, just as a memento.'

'No.'

I took the box out of his hand. I didn't even think, this was something of Max's I wanted. It was skilfully worked, and it might contain a secret. I was thinking of a suicide note. A last intimate connection with my brother.

'I think he'd have wanted me to have it,' Stephen said.

'Why?'

Our spikiness was turning to open hostility.

'Thing is,' he went on, an edge of strain in his voice, 'thing is, I'm wondering what's inside it. Have you noticed? There's something inside it.' He took the box back from me and shook it. 'Max liked the last word.'

We both stared at the brick. In an ideal world we'd now find a way to open it, we'd look inside together, and discover Max's note. We'd read it together, and bond over its warm words. Stephen held it, turned it over, fingered it.

'If there's a message in there it'll be for me,' I said.

His eyes flickered towards mine, then away.

'There's no point my staying here,' I said.

'In this house?'

'In this country. I've missed the funeral.' I found I was almost spitting these four words, furious with myself. I took a breath. 'I might as well go straight home.'

'OK. But do you want to see the grave? I'll take you.'

I nodded. 'Give me a few minutes.'

As the door shut I sank on to the bed, thinking about that bayonet, Max asleep with his hand draped over it, as if prepared to defend himself from the world full of strangers outside his front door. Should have tried harder with Stephen, but somehow I couldn't be bothered. He seemed to feel the same way with me. I wasn't sure if the situation was retrievable, but perhaps I should try donating a story to him, as an offering of friendship.

When I was twelve, I skinned a cat. A dead one. It

belonged to a friend and I told her I'd bury it for her, because she was so upset. She brought it round in a shoebox, and I solemnly took it, and assured her I'd give it a decent burial. I took it into the garden with a trowel, rubber gloves, a handkerchief and a sharp kitchen knife. Just curious. I'd seen it done by Alan Ladd, with a buffalo. I pulled on the pink rubber gloves, put the handkerchief over my mouth and nose, and started in the middle of the spine. I stabbed the cat, worked the blade under the skin, then moved it in a sawing motion towards the head. Pushing against unexpectedly tough resistance, discovering the wet, red world under the skin.

I kept trying, out of stubbornness, for perhaps three minutes. Then I looked at the mess I'd made and started to cry. I stuck the trowel into the earth and dug and dug, then dropped the heavy, bloody shoe-box into the hole I'd made. Scooped the earth back over it and stamped it down, apologising all the time. That's me. Liable to make a mess, but usually there with a hopeful, futile apology.

I sat in Max's room, retelling that old secret story to myself, wondering what Stephen would make of it. He might be shocked, but I would tell him that everyone lives the same way, nursing secret stories, developing layers. Hidden melancholy in the blood. He might say not everyone has skinned a cat, but I'd reply not everyone receives anonymous, accusatory letters. I wondered what Stephen was hiding behind his stories, his strained manner, that distance. This is where being easier with people might help — small talk, flirting, eye-contact, finally earnest conversation, digging, digging. If I was better at all that I'd be able to get under his skin, gain his confidence, learn his secrets. I remembered the letter. *You could start by telling the truth, that would be novel.*

What was he lying about?

Human Watching

I T   W A S   Q U I E T upstairs. Gloria collecting herself before the trip to the cemetery. Stephen read and reread Jude's letters. He had decided they were from Jude, although the postcodes and the type-written messages gave no clue. There were simply no other suspects. Great. This was all he needed. Max dead, his pissed-off sister setting fire to the kitchen, and now this ghost from the past sending him vicious letters.

If he'd known Gloria much longer he might have suspected her of sending them. Somehow they'd already nettled each other. That dismissive nod when he'd said what he'd planned to say about getting to know each other, as if she couldn't care less about him. That had started it. And then the argument over Max's piece. And her distant manner. Maybe she was distracted by grief, maybe they both were, but he'd be glad when she left. He had a feeling that she was a few steps to one side on the sanity scale. And she'd been reading the letters when he came in. Did that mean she'd blame him?

He tapped the paper, dragged his fingertips across it as if he might detect some clue on its surface. Rachel was a possibility. Maybe there was something a bit mad about her too. Red lips, screwed curls, a sense always of something behind her face. She certainly had a grudge over the way he'd ended it. He held the paper up to the light, as if a watermark might reveal everything. Not

Rachel. He couldn't see her doing something so covert. The wine in the face was more her speed. He flinched at the thought of it. He sometimes felt that women's grasp of the ordinary flow of life was more tenuous than men's That was the problem with Rachel. And Katie, with her unsuitable lovers. It was perhaps also behind the friction with Gloria.

He came back, inevitably, to Jude. He'd had two years with her, which was his record, before it ended so badly. She couldn't cope, she'd finally explained, with his moods, and with what she called his hapless quality; she wanted a more settled man in her life. Women get away with saying stuff like that because they're meant to be good at empathy and talking. Men are meant to blunder through relationships, uncommunicative, quietly angry.

Gloria came in and Stephen glared at her.

'All right,' she said, misunderstanding. 'I read your letters.'

'I know.' He folded them and pushed them back into his pocket. 'I'm not angry with you, I was thinking of something else.'

'What?'

'Never mind.'

'Is it about the letters? Who's sending them, do you know?'

'A woman called Jude, I think.'

'Tell me about her.'

'No.'

Gloria stared at him. 'She says you know why he did it.'

'She's wrong.'

Gloria stared, he stared back. Communication was proving difficult. Jude, Rachel, now Gloria.

And Stephen, by the way, you're a disaster with women.

❧

Mike, wearing overalls and shaded goggles, is welding something to his sculpture. This is a large, hideous thing, involving a couple of bits of scaffolding, a scaly hand, a pulley, and bits and pieces like old ashtrays and a torch. As Simon enters Mike pauses and takes off his goggles.

SIMON Can't you do that somewhere else? Seriously, do it somewhere else. What is it about our front room?

MIKE: It's the light.

SIMON: You get light in a studio, you only need a window.

MIKE: I can't work with sub-standard light.

SIMON: Sub-standard?

MIKE: I need light that's limpid, lucid, thin and transparent.

SIMON: I know, that thick, opaque light's a bastard, isn't it?

MIKE: Rose been complaining?

Simon doesn't answer.

MIKE: She knew I was part of the deal when she moved in.

SIMON: Why are we talking about Rose?

MIKE: Things not going well?

SIMON: I can't always . . . I find it hard . . . I can't always get through.

No answer.

SIMON: OK, you know in *Star Trek*, they have a Universal Translator? It's like we're using one of those but it's faulty, so I say something and she hears something slightly different, and she answers, but she's responding to something I haven't said.

MIKE: *Star Trek.*
SIMON: It's a simile.
Mike shakes his head, pulls down his goggles and starts welding again.
SIMON: What?

Saturday afternoon, blandly pleasant weather. It wasn't happiness I was feeling, but there was some satisfaction in moving among the peaceful trees and tombstones. A cool breeze, flat, firm light over everything, the rustle of water nearby, falling over stones. Stephen had thickly-haired forearms. The hair spread right up the back of his hands and up to the first knuckle of his fingers. I'd been looking as we drove here, without much else to do. We were barely speaking.

We walked down a gravel path, heading towards the central green hub. Stones stretched away on all sides. Stubby traditional ones like milestones, rectangular ones like pieces of paving, crosses, long flat slabs, angels and doves, and big stone blocks like family-size freezers. I was feeling more relaxed now. I left Stephen on his direct route to the grave. I read one stone and then another until I was tempted off the path, like a child in a fairy tale, into the thick of the dead crowd.

Stephen waited as I meandered.

FENELLA WRIGHT had PASSED AWAY the year before, at twenty-six. Fenella, according to her stone, was DEEPLY MISSED by her parents and her brother. I guessed at leukaemia. Her brother had probably donated his bone marrow, but it hadn't taken, or had been too late. He'd feel, at least, that he'd done all he could for her. At the end, the family would have been allowed to remove the masks and gloves that protected Fenella from their infections, there'd have been a moving exchange of tears, kisses and good byes.

After further detours I arrived, finally, at Max's grave. Brushing past Stephen, I stood on it deliberately, heels sinking a little into the dishevelled earth.

'I've ordered the stone. You can contact them about the inscription.' Stephen was whispering.

Who did he think he was going to disturb? Max in his box, underground? I laid the carnations I'd brought on the earth. They were white, spattered with red, uncomfortably like blood, I now thought.

'Could you, just for a minute, leave me alone?'

I sensed hesitation, but he went. I'd pulled rank, asserted my place in the hierarchy of grief. He wandered off, leaving me heel-deep in grave dirt, staring at where the stone should be, trying to find fit thoughts for the occasion. Nothing at first, except intense regret about missing the funeral, as if somehow if I'd been there it would have made a difference. Then an image of Max's face; then a memory of him in the sea, knee-deep and swearing at the waves; another of his kiss good bye when I was leaving for Hong Kong, his cheek next to mine as if he was looking away, over my shoulder.

After a while, I had a strange impulse. I glanced around, then crouched as if to look more closely at something. I searched my pocket for some coins, then dropped them on to the earth between my shoes, pushed them a little, so they infiltrated the loose soil. Then I remained crouching there above the buried coins, getting a faint smell of carnations, and a stronger one of fresh, damp earth.

As I straightened I saw, half a field away, some cars unloading a flock of mourners. None were looking my way, they were milling, waiting for their coffin to emerge.

I spotted Stephen and headed quickly towards him, with an eye on the funeral party.

'Come on,' I said, reaching him.

'What?' said Stephen. But he followed me as we approached the darkly-dressed group gathering behind the coffin. We hurried discreetly between the graves until we were tagging along with the last of the mourners, a pony-tailed man and his wife.

'What are you doing?' Stephen hissed.

I ignored him.

'He were a *bas*tard, but you couldn't help liking him.'

This from pony tail, pushing his fingers through his hair.

'Sssh,' said his wife.

'You've got to be clear-eyed about it, though,' I told her.

My instinct was, if you're going to gatecrash a funeral, you should do so with conviction.

'She's right.' Pony tail again. 'Otherwise, what's the point?'

'You've got to be truthful, haven't you?' I said to Stephen. He was glaring at me again.

The wife looked at us. She wore a lilac suit, and a hat with a bundle of black crepe pinned on top of it.

'Who are you?'

Was there a touch of suspicion in her tone? I heard Stephen suck in a breath. 'Friends,' I said, confidently. 'From abroad.'

She nodded like this made sense, apparently satisfied.

'Malta,' said Pony tail. He nodded at me too, and his eyes slipped from my face to my chest. 'Peter,' he said.

'I'm Marion,' said his wife. 'It's a sad day.'

That seemed to be enough, we'd been accepted.

The vicar marshalled us around the hole and we stood

at the back with our two new friends. A young woman and a young man in a wheelchair flanked the widow at the graveside. Stephen hissed something at me again, but I wasn't listening. I felt the air move on my face, heard the river again, and then I looked at the long brown box, trying not to imagine Max's body inside it. Partly because Max's body must have been a horrendous mess, and partly because of a little shiver of claustrophobia. Ever since seeing a film called *The Vanishing*, in which a man is buried alive, I'd known I wanted to be cremated when the time came. Cremated and, if possible, shot into space.

The vicar said his words, the daughter added a stuttering postscript, the box was lowered and a few fistfuls of earth were dropped. I looked away, staring at the tall trees at the edge of the cemetery, conjuring Max's face again.

Creases around his eyes and forehead, his lips in an impatient pout. He said, 'Come on, come on, get up here.'

He was sitting in a tall tree, on a branch well away from the trunk, legs dangling over the drop below.

'Are you scared? Don't be scared, what's the point?'

'I don't want to fall, that's the point,' I said.

But I climbed the rope ladder anyway, grazing my knuckles and bruising my knees, not looking down, listening to my agitated breaths. I got level with Max's branch. It was as far as I'd ever got.

'Shuffle over. Hang on to the ladder and stretch your leg on to the branch.'

'Don't want to.'

'Trust me, you'll be fine.'

He was eleven, I was eight. I was used to trusting him. I didn't fancy this, though.

'Do it, or I won't be your friend any more.'

'What?'

'I mean it.'

All I saw in his face was his usual conviction. I believed him. So I did it. Clutched the rope ladder with my right hand, hugged the tree with my left arm, and stretched first one leg then the other on to the branch.

'OK, OK, I'm doing it,' I was whispering.

'See. Easy,' he said. Then suddenly he was standing on the branch, making it bounce alarmingly, holding on to the branch above and walking towards me, then round me. Then he was going down the ladder.

'Bye!'

I sat on my precarious perch, trembling and crying, and watched him run away from me, laughing, back to the house.

The trees I was staring at moved in the breeze. Stephen fidgeted and I ignored him, tuning back in to the present. I could almost believe this was Max's funeral, and I was thinking it was right, what they say about the usefulness of ritual. The gathering together, the sing-song of the vicar, the choice of dark clothes, the self-conscious words of the bereaved, it all felt like a necessary response, and it was what I had missed. Now people were kissing each other and tears were being shed. I was shedding them again, trembling and crying. Maybe it was odd to latch on to this stranger's funeral, maybe it was wrong, but it was answering a need. Stephen extended those cautious fingers towards me again, but it was Marion who put an arm round me. I smelt sweet, syrupy stuff on her neck and wrists. Stephen lowered his hand, stood stiffly beside me as I wept.

Marion asked would they see us at the funeral tea? Stephen said No, and I said Yes.

'Oh good,' she said. 'You can take us.'

Stephen pulled me aside and whispered savagely, 'Tell

them.' I turned my tear-blotched face at him and said mildly, 'I'm doing this. I want to.' Then I linked my arm in Marion's and led her to his car, leaving him to follow with pony-tailed Peter.

We arrived first, with James, in his wheelchair, and his sister. The four of us waited in the sitting room as Marion and Peter disappeared. Sofa in ridged red material, rough to the touch. TV. A table surrounded by stiff-backed chairs, laid with cakes and sandwiches. Bottles and glasses lined on a sideboard. The walls were bright blue, and the colour scheme on the whole was clownish, insistently jolly.

Stephen sat down, his jaw set so that it looked like he was clenching his teeth. He looked at me, and I looked away. I didn't know what I was doing. I didn't know what the coins in the earth were about, and I was afraid that at any moment Stephen and I would be exposed. It was as if I was being kidnapped again, but by someone who didn't know where they wanted to go and had no set goal in mind, just needed to be in motion.

Thumps overhead as others washed and pissed, preparing for the second phase of the rite. They'd been solemn, and now they were going to be happy.

'That lilac, a mistake.' Words came with difficulty to James, squeezed past his resistant jaw and tongue.

'You want creamy skin for lilac,' I agreed. 'She's too flushed.'

'Looks like,' he said, 'a bruise.'

His sister laughed. 'James,' she breathed, as if he'd said something shocking. She looked at us apologetically. 'He's very rude.'

James and I were eyeing each other as she spoke.

'Who are you?' he said.

'From Malta.'

I sensed Stephen shifting a little, next to me.

'How did you know,' James gasped, 'Dad?'

The door swung open and Peter and Marion came in. Peter patted her bum and winked at me. 'Everyone ship-shape?' He swivelled away towards the drinks.

As the room filled, Stephen got talking to James's sister, who he probably considered fairly safe. I hovered near James, watching. Men were mostly matey with him, women mostly maternal. Two children approached him, dressed like a boy and a girl in a miniature suit and a puffy frock, but not yet old enough to split neatly into matey or maternal. They were just curious.

'Why do you speak like that?'

'Why can't you stand up?'

James answered as well as he could, explaining that he'd been in a car accident, and then their mother swept them up, giving him a solicitous smile as she did so. I took their place, sitting beside him, and praised his patience. He said that in a different mood he'd have blamed his condition on wolves. For a while after that we observed the cat's cradle of glances around the room, listening to the chatter, hearing nuances of tone.

'You watch,' he said.

'Yes.'

'Me too. Human watching. Peter, shagging her. You think?' He nodded at another woman, not Marion.

I nodded too. 'Probably.'

'Whose grave were you at, today?'

I looked at him, but couldn't read his expression.

'My brother's,' I said.

He paused. I wasn't sure if he was finding it hard to speak, or if he was angry.

'What did you do?' he said. 'When you knelt?'

'Left some coins in the earth. I wanted to leave

something there. I missed his funeral.' The words sounded pathetic and inadequate. 'Then I saw you, and I wanted to be involved. I shouldn't be here, I'm sorry.'

James looked at me for a few moments. 'Don't be sorry,' he said.

Some more silence between us. Comfortable, this time. We were human watching again, but I was aware of physical presences as well as the social dynamic. During my year in Hong Kong I'd begun to feel bulky and much too tall. Now, although I was an interloper here, I was beginning to realise I was home again.

I watched Stephen sinking a beer. He glanced at me, then back at James's sister. He seemed more at ease.

'You can smell,' said James. 'As well as watch.'

We sat there for several minutes. I smelt the breath of an old uncle, which was like a room you haven't entered for a long time; apple shampoo; the talcumy yawn of an opened handbag; sour body odour; a whiff of urine, either from a little girl or that same old uncle. Meanwhile several people talked briefly to James, plates of food precariously balanced. They all said it was a lovely ceremony, and most of them added that his father was a good man. Then there was a pause and they moved on, with a curious nod at me.

'Look.'

I followed James's eyes towards Stephen, who was still with his sister, but was now darting impatient glances at me.

'He's in there.' James's laugh was like a guttural cough. A couple of people looked round, worried. 'Your boyfriend?'

His eyes appraised me more honestly than Peter's or Stephen's.

'No,' I said. 'And we have to go, I'm afraid. I hope we didn't intrude?'

He shook his head vigorously. 'You and me,' he said, 'both mourning. Most of these . . .' His unsteady hand shook at the room.

I stood and kissed him. 'Thanks, then.'

'Come back,' he said.

Stephen watched them kiss. It wasn't much, but it lasted a couple of seconds, and Gloria had definitely initiated it. She bent and her lips pressed on the corner of James's mouth. She smiled at him, and he at her. Peter's eyes were on her breast, squashing briefly on James's shoulder. He winked at Stephen again.

Stephen looked away, wondering why he hadn't kissed Gloria yet. He'd barely touched her. He wanted to hold her and feel a strong current of sympathy passing between them. He thought it would be something physical, like a shudder, or a sudden warmth. Instead, just this wariness, as if each feared the other carried a disease.

Growing up, Max and I were slow to learn the knack of making friends. We tried too hard or, more often, didn't try at all. A childhood sense that meeting people was difficult had hardened into a firm belief that it was an ordeal, best avoided. I was surprised to realise I'd made a good impression on James.

I nodded at him. 'I will.'

We got out fairly smoothly. I turned my cheek to a kiss from Peter and stepped away from his hands. He smelt of tobacco and aftershave.

Stephen was silent in the car for the first few minutes.

'I've been to a funeral now,' I said. 'I feel a bit better. I might stay another day or two.'

'Long as you like.'

'I could go to a hotel, but I'd like to be where Max was.'

'Of course.'

'And if I'm staying, I want to meet people Max knew, get a sense of how he lived. I want to, if possible, know why he did it. And don't argue with me, we both know he killed himself.' I realised I was almost quoting one of Stephen's letters. 'All I want is the whole story.'

Stephen stared at me. 'Stay,' he said finally. 'We can sort out,' a wave of the hand, 'everything.'

Meaning, presumably, that we could argue later about who Max would have wanted to own his brick. Discuss how to get at its contents without taking an axe to it. Raise the question of the anonymous letters. Investigate the unexpected sketch of Rachel we'd found in his room.

He dug in his pocket, eyes on the road, found Max's key and gave it to me. He dropped it into my palm as if avoiding contact with my skin.

I looked at him. 'Are you angry with me?'

He was still watching the road and for a moment I thought he wasn't going to answer.

Finally, he said, 'Just wondering what you're going to do next.'

Box

W HAT I DID NEXT was buy some food and cook for both of us. I chopped peppers, garlic, onion and courgettes and pushed them round a pan, imagining Max moving round this kitchen, imagining him standing beside me and leaning round me to smell the food. I added ginger, bean curd, water chestnuts. Stephen had gone out to buy a bottle of white wine. This was all in the spirit of starting again — nothing had been said, but we were both feeling it, wanting to see if we could wipe out the abrasive edge that was between us. I'd slept after the funeral and was fresher, although no clearer about the future. Colourful green and red vegetables sizzled and spat. I inhaled the smells, looking forward to a drink, feeling almost normal for the first time since I'd arrived.

Max was beside me, and he was in my head. Big brother, telling me he was shrinking along with me, sitting on the end of my bed after Dad died, in the bedroom with the hooded mirror, talking it through. Abandoning me up the tree and seeming to think he deserved my thanks for forcing me up there. Later, reassuring me after Mike Harper chucked me; driving me to a cinema or home from a party; being in some ways the parent that my mother couldn't be, and being so gravely nice to the girls I knew that they all fell for him. But moving away from me, increasingly distant, wrapped up in himself and a world I only guessed at. I guessed at drugs and failed exams and careless relationships. I forgot the trial it was for him to get to know people, I forgot the gravity that weighed him down, and the deep, sad core of self-involvement that was always going to be unsatisfied.

There was a period, not long after he'd finished with school, when he spent a lot of time underground. Our garage was under the house and it became Max's first workshop. I'd get sent down with messages from Mum, something feeble and vague like: 'Tell him I want him.' I'd abandon my A level revision and head down, feeling like I was visiting a troll in his cave.

One time, I found Max bent over an oddly-shaped block of stone, raising puffs of dust with his chisel. Usually when I disturbed him he'd stop working immediately, as if caught doing something embarrassing, so I stood a while in the doorway, silent, watching. His attention to the stone wasn't absolute. He had a radio on, and he turned and adjusted the tuning. Then he stepped back and scratched himself, looked at the ceiling, then approached the stone again and hammered it. I wasn't sure if it was frustration or artistic choice. Two hard chops with the chisel and then some delicate taps with another tool.

'You going to stand there all day?' he said, without turning to me.

'I didn't want to disturb you.'

'Then why you here?'

'Mum needs you.'

'Can't you deal with her?'

All this with his back to me, addressing the bit of stone in front of him.

'What is that?' I said.

'Nothing, yet.'

This is how it often was with Max. You'd try to talk to him and he'd be unfriendly, uncooperative, apparently waiting for you to leave. Mum was supposed to be the ill one, but Max was often more difficult.

He dropped the chisel and turned to me finally.

'No,' he said, as if we were discussing it, 'I'm glad you're interrupting me, interruption is what I need.'

And suddenly he had his hands on my shoulders.

'Let's see what Mum wants. I don't know about her, I need a drink. Have we got a drink in the house?'

And then he was out of the garage, running up the steps to the house, me following more slowly, and it was all right, he was relaxed, he could cope with everything, his bad mood forgotten.

Max beside me in the kitchen. Smelling the food. *What, no meat?* I put an arm round him, as if to stop him running away. I said, 'I'm sorry about your friend, it's awful for you, but at least it's brought us together.'

Stephen came back with the wine, I served up, we sat down, and then we both waited for conversation to begin. He said something complimentary about the food. I raised an aromatic forkful towards my mouth. Thanked him. More waiting. I could hear his jaw moving, crushing bean sprouts. I needed to speak soon, if only to cover that sound.

'Any more stories about Max?'

'Not happy ones.'

'Tell me.'

Stephen hesitated, sipped wine, making his choice. I hated him for a second, for his deliberation, his experience of Max, the power it gave him.

'Did you know he had a job last winter?'

I shook my head, trying to ignore the swell of anger I felt. Starting again, starting again. He's doing his best, and he's grieving as I am. I don't wish him dead. I don't wish him dead.

'Max had this job, just temporary, to pay the rent. I think he quite enjoyed it for a while.'

'And they sacked him?'

'No.' Stephen looked less rehearsed this time. He wasn't seeing me, he was seeing Max, and it brought a liveliness to his voice.

'He's answering the phone, photocopying, taking pieces of paper from one department to another, exchanging chat with secretaries. The agency sent him there for two weeks, but he'd been there ten because work kept accumulating, springing from somewhere. By the third month it's just papers appearing in his tray and Max transferring the data on to his screen. On his left, Will doing the same thing. On his right, Chloe also doing the same thing. The paper accumulating in their trays, and the three of them dealing with it.'

I glanced at Stephen. Now the liveliness was fading and he looked distant and serious, like a doctor delivering a troubling diagnosis.

'He said it was easy to be in the office. Talking to Will and Chloe and not talking to them, arriving late and stretching the lunch hour and leaving early. So he's somewhere in the third month and there's no sign of it ending. He's in the office, sitting at his terminal, moving information, when suddenly he's standing up. He feels his heart beating.

'Tell them I'm sick,' he says to Chloe, and Chloe says 'What?' and he says 'Tell them anything.'

'He's walking out of the office, and then he's running to the lift, and when it doesn't come he runs down the stairs, tears in his eyes by this time, and he's running nowhere in particular except out of the building and away, through the streets, away from the office. He arrives at some terrible pub, goes to the toilet and kneels in front of it, throws up his lunch and then sits down, trying to breathe, trying to breathe deep and slow, his heart racing so he thinks he's going to die.'

Stephen glanced briefly at me. Looked away. He seemed to be outlining a shape, with his hands in front of his face. Something massy and round. 'He said it was like when the coyote runs off the edge of the cliff and keeps running, until he looks down. Then he sees where he is, sees that he's hanging in thin air, and he falls.'

I refilled my glass. The wine was flowery, but there was a sour edge to it. Cheap. 'It's not a story, exactly,' I said. 'It's just a thing that happened.'

'What's the difference?'

'It's just a thing that Max did. He was depressed one day and he left his job.'

He looked at me. 'What more do you want?'

'I want everything. I want to know all about him.'

He almost laughed. 'Everything.'

Our attempt to be friendly was stuttering. If Max was alive, our conversation might have been forced, but we'd have tried to get to know each other peaceably, tried to become friends for his sake. Now we seemed unable to speak without disagreeing.

'That's why I have to talk to people who knew him,' I said, aiming for a mild tone. 'I can't just rely on your version. I told you, I need the whole story.' I was trying to convey the short, sharp facts of the matter. 'I didn't know about his job, because I didn't know him. So I need to find out what was happening in his head. Why he did it.'

Stephen stared at me. 'We still don't know that he killed himself.'

This was out of nowhere, and surprised me.

'We do.'

I wondered if he was saying it for my benefit.

Stephen leant forward, eager and unpersuasive. He'd spent some time, I realised, trying to convince himself.

'First, no witnesses,' he said. 'Second, something about Max you may not have seen—he liked to clown. He'd walk along the tops of walls, jump down half a flight of stairs.'

'Two things. I grew up with Max, I have seen him walk along walls, climb trees. And no witnesses? What about the train driver?'

'Inconclusive. All he knew was suddenly there was . . . there was a body.'

'So you think Max was, what? Clowning? Trying to jump from one platform to the other, when suddenly this train he hadn't noticed shows up?'

'No, I don't know. I just don't think it's certain.'

'Stephen, it's certain.'

'For instance, if there was an animal on the track. I wouldn't put it past him to go down there to rescue it.'

'Oh, please. Are we back to cats?'

Silence. Start again. For a while there was nothing to hear but more crunching of bean sprouts and peppers. I wasn't clear about the future, but I knew I didn't want to spend too many evenings in a red kitchen with an unfriendly stranger.

I finished my last forkful of rice. Wondered what on earth we were going to do next.

'Do you want to go out?' said Stephen.

I looked sceptical.

'Maybe a club.'

This was something else he had planned.

'What should I wear?'

He looked at me and one side of his mouth moved

towards a smile. 'Black is fine. I'll call Katie, a friend of Max's. You'll want to meet her.'

One of Max's favourite places, apparently. I felt a sagging in my stomach as I stood in the harsh light of the bathroom, putting a Saturday-night face on, feeling no bright premonitions for the evening ahead. I hadn't realised grief could be such a physical sensation. I wanted to go to one of Max's favourite places with Max. I was expecting some smoky little jazz hole. Stephen and Katie would probably be aficionados, in that boring, cool way. And Katie would be curious, probably disapproving. Stephen would warn her on the phone, *She says she hardly even knew him. Don't know how long she's staying. You'll never guess—she gate-crashed a funeral.* I stared in the mirror. Wished Clara was with me. On good days I felt blonde, felt I had a lustre about me. On other days I felt pale and lank. I was heavy on the mascara and the eyeliner, then pouted aggressively while applying bruise-coloured lipstick, thinking of James.

Fat Greg on the plane, Robbie the aggressive hitcher in his ugly anorak, James in his wheelchair, and awkward, unpromising Stephen—my unlikely address book was expanding every day. I need my life peopled, I'd told Clara. Did these four count?

We drove along wide, dull A-roads to Bradford, as light turned slowly to dark. Stephen had on a black denim jacket. There was a vertical line between his eyebrows as he peered at the road ahead, and a delta of wrinkles at the corner of each eye. He ran a hand through his short hair and glanced at me, sensing my gaze on him. I smiled briefly, looked away. Katie couldn't make it, apparently. Something about some man she was with. She'd see me tomorrow. He'd tried not to sound disappointed when he told me, but it was clear he'd been looking forward to having an ally.

Street lamps came on, pink at first, then orange, glowing like heating filaments. We got lost in a sprawling, godforsaken estate for a while, driving in large, uneven circles, watched by bands of kids on corners. My mood sinking. I spotted a number plate on a parked car. *Traveller Goes Missing*. I didn't mention it, stayed patiently quiet, aware of the brittle atmosphere. Men in cars hate to lose their way. Then we spilled off the estate, randomly I guessed, and Stephen shoved an *A-Z* at me and asked me, in a voice straining to be casual, to look up Hangingroyd Lane.

Promising name, I thought, but didn't say.

We parked eventually outside a sex shop, in the window of which a busty mannequin was wearing studded leather knickers. It was dark now and as soon as I got out of the car I smelt sewage, like it was a transparent fog hanging in the air. One of those edgy streets where eyes watch you, and you wouldn't want to be there on your own. Maybe Stephen was getting some buzz from his role, escorting me. I gave the boys across the road my hard stare and imagined Max walking this street. I could see how he'd have liked it, curious and unintimidated, with a bounce in his stride like he was hoping someone might challenge him.

No bounce in Stephen's stride. He led me quickly past the sex shop and down some steps, beneath dull silver letters on a crooked sign. BOX. Of course it had to be a basement, of course it had to be dark. From the neck down I was probably invisible.

Stephen bought us beers and we sat at a table. He was watching me, waiting for my reaction, so I looked around, trying to do it in a cool way. For a start, there were cameras everywhere. I tuned-in to the sound that had been bothering me — a low buzz, the just-audible techno-whine of offices. A camera angled towards me.

'We're on the net,' Stephen said. 'Clubcam. Twenty-four hours a day.'

Ho hum. Perhaps we'd meet Greg here. In a corner, in a pool of light, another camera was focused on a woman who was writing on a wall already thickly covered with words. She seemed to be copying from a fat book. I looked enquiringly at Stephen.

'She's copying the *OED* on to the wall of the club. Every word is going to be mis-spelt. She says she's reinventing the language.'

A smile in his voice. I could see Max and Stephen sat at this table. Max would make caustic comments and Stephen would smirk. It would be better than the red kitchen.

He nodded. 'Look over there.'

A long, closed box, like a coffin. Above it there was a TV monitor with a man's face on it.

'There's a guy nailed in the box with a camera on him. He gets water and rice cakes passed through a slot, and he does three day shifts, with his partner. The piece is called Tank. This whole place is an ongoing installation, that's the idea.'

I looked at the TV, at the face of the man in the box. Still and colourless. I tried to read some expression from the clear image. There was a hint of discomfort perhaps, in the purse of his mouth.

Stephen was watching me watching. 'I heard he cut off one of his own fingers.'

'He what?'

'Cut it off and ate it.'

'Now you're joking.'

He shrugged. 'That's what I heard.'

'And Max's feelings about this place?'

Stephen shook his head. 'Hard to say. It had a sort of fascination.'

'Wasn't he irritated? People with adolescent ideas and no talent, pretending to be artists?'

'I couldn't tell.' Stephen drained his beer. 'I couldn't tell.'

'You should have asked.'

Suddenly he looked irritated. Leant across the table, pushing his face towards me.

'I was hoping,' he said, 'that we'd get on.'

'But?'

'But since you got here you've shouted at a stranger, thrown-up, read my letters, gate-crashed someone's funeral, and treated me like an inconvenience.'

'What did you want? Someone who'd cry gratefully on your shoulder?'

I felt on the verge of shouting at him, having a stand-up, throwing-things row with him, because I had a big bed of anger close to the surface, close to eruption, and I knew there was something similar in him too, a pressure there, a readiness to be affronted. But what he said was true, and there was the man with his urn, and Greg on the plane, and the encounter with Robbie hadn't been very friendly. I'd hoped when I left Hong Kong that I might start afresh, invent a new Gloria, someone gregarious and tolerant. Apart from my brief connection with James, which was down to him, not me, I'd made no progress at all. It was beginning to feel like I was out to offend all the men I met, like it was a project.

My breath was ragged and shallow but I didn't shout, and neither did Stephen. We stared at each other for a few seconds, full of frank dislike, and then the music suddenly started, loud and throbbing.

'Come on.' I pulled Stephen off his seat, his weight sagged and resisted a moment and then he was up and on to the small dance floor with me and we started to move in the blaring sound that vibrated the walls.

Cameras whirred towards us. Around the world men watched us on their high-res screens, underground in Bradford in the dark. Stephen, to my surprise, was up for it. He rippled his arms at me and I shimmied my hips towards him, shoulders tilting from side to side. We seemed to fit, the way it sometimes happens with a man you don't like. The woman kept writing on the wall in felt tip. The man in the box absently nodded his head in time to the beat. It felt good to do something physical and thoughtless. I danced as if it was fifteen years earlier, as if Stephen was an exciting new man in my life, as if the future was clear as water, and nothing but hopeful.

I even thought about sex with him, and it briefly seemed desirable. To forget myself and Max, to replace our awkwardness and aggression with excitement. I couldn't imagine this feeling continuing, once the music had stopped.

When something more dissonant and less danceable came on, we fell back into our seats, tired and sweaty. I swallowed half a bottle of beer and talked at Stephen. I had difficulty making myself heard over the music. Communication always seemed to be like this: awkward, stunted, misunderstood.

'I'm coming to see Jude with you,' I shouted.

'I'm not going to see her.'

'She was writing about my brother. I told you, I want to meet people he knew.'

'One, it's private, and two, I'm just going to forget about it.'

The music stopped abruptly and my next words were shouted into silence.

'What have you been lying about?'

Stephen's stony face stared at me.

Then I drank too much. It became one of those nights when after a while you don't know what you're feeling, whether your brain is clear or fuzzy, whether you're happy or sad. At one point I thought I was still on the plane, between places, several thousand feet up. I can't remember what we talked about. I remember saying, earnestly, as if Stephen needed persuading, 'Max was marvellous, and when he died the shine went out of everything.' And I remember saying, 'Stephen, can I say something? I think at this point, I should say this. Clear the air.' He just looked at me, eyebrows up. 'No offence, but you are nothing like the kind of man I would want to sleep with.' That was while we were dancing again. I smiled at him and touched his cheek, to soften the blow, if it was a blow. He'd missed a little patch of bristle by the corner of his mouth. And I remember that as Stephen led me out I thumped on the box where the man with a missing finger lay and shouted at him, 'Get out of the box, you tosser!'

I remember our last exchange perfectly. We sat in the car in the dark street. The cold air had sobered me up a bit. After a few minutes I realised we weren't moving.

'Why aren't we moving?'

Stephen had his hands on the wheel and was staring at the road as if he was driving.

'Maybe Max and I should never have gone there,' he said, eventually. 'Maybe we should have found better ways to spend our time.'

I shook my head. 'Wasting your time's all right now and then. Trust me, I'm an expert, I've just wasted a whole year.'

'And you're happy with that?'

'No,' I drawled the word scornfully. It made me remember how much I'd drunk, how jet lag still had me off-balance. 'Happiness only turns up now and then, for a few moments. There's a giant Buddha on Lantau island. I went there with Clara. And Scarborough. Max and me used to go to Scarborough, did he tell you?'

'No.'

'That was good for happy moments.'

He looked interested, like a happiness-historian, like now might be the ideal time for him to hear all about our family holidays, centuries ago.

He glanced at me, realised I wasn't going to elaborate, then watched the road again.

'I wanted us to get on.'

'You said that.'

'I'm a good teacher, and I live in a nice place, but my life at the moment, ever since Jude, my life is . . .' He trailed off.

'Shit. I know. I guessed. So's mine.'

He didn't answer. Two days together and we were running out of words.

'Maybe Max had the right idea,' I said. 'Killing himself.'

He stared at me. I could see he was wondering what to say. Then he started the car. I slept fitfully all the way home and dreamt that Stephen had hijacked my car and was driving me somewhere. A stand of tall trees was involved, Stephen and I were digging with our bare hands among the roots, and Max looked down at us from a high branch, laughing.

Sunday

About Jude

'STEPHEN'S NO HELP, he feels guilty.'
Katie nodded. 'But we all do, don't we?'

I gave her a coffee, suddenly I was the host, and we went through to the sitting room. There was a foggy Sunday morning laziness about us, much less effort than with Stephen.

'Someone suggested a Bereavement Management class,' I told her. It had been Clara, trying to manage not so much my bereavement, as me. 'She said there'll be stages. Denial, Anger, Grief, Recovery.'

'Was she right?'

'No. It's more Confusion, Baths, Talking.'

Katie sipped coffee. 'Sounds healthier.'

I'd come downstairs in a dressing gown, looking for aspirin, and the doorbell had rung. I'd opened the door and Katie had hugged me, just like Clara a few days earlier. 'Gloria,' she'd said, arms around me, 'I'm so sorry.' It was lovely, some uncomplicated female warmth. I'd hugged her back, thanked her, asked if she knew where the aspirin were.

'It's Jude we need to talk to,' I said. 'She at least thinks she knows something.'

Katie looked sceptical.

'All right,' I said, hitting the table with the side of my hand. 'Whoever's sending the letters knows why Max killed himself. Yes? Stephen says Jude's sending them. We go and see Jude, and she tells us why Max is dead.'

Katie shook her head. 'Stephen said he never wanted to see Jude again, ever.'

'Why?'

Katie sighed. 'I shouldn't.'

'Come on.'

So she took a deep breath and told the story.

Stephen, Max and Katie had reached the Registry Office at ten to three and were shown into a waiting room by a woman in a pale blue sequinned dress. Stephen in his suit, talking more than usual.

He said, 'This is the age we're at. Marriage. It's the next step.'

He bummed one of Katie's fags and they went outside again where he started pacing like a stressed businessman. Max watched him, Katie said, 'Relax, will you?'

Stephen stopped pacing. 'Because at a certain point you say: *What am I for?* And you realise it's time to start shaping your life into something. Into a shape.'

Katie smoothed her silvery dress over her thighs. 'Are you having a go at us now?'

'No, I'm really glad you're here, you two. I wanted my best friends here.' He checked his watch. 'I'm just saying this is right for me.'

They went inside again and a noisy party appeared, flowing past the door of the waiting room in a blur of colours and flowers and kisses. He watched them, trying to look pleased and calm in case one of them looked in.

Max had his legs stretched out, crossed at the ankle. 'You don't get shape in your life,' he said, 'till you're old and you look back. If then.'

'I don't even want shape in my life,' said Katie.

'She should be here.' Stephen checked his watch again. 'Shouldn't she be here by now?'

They sat a while longer and the mood slowly changed. Katie ran out of reassurances, Max grew more silent. The sequinned woman arrived in the doorway, looked at the three of them, went away again.

Stephen borrowed Katie's mobile. He sat angled slightly away from Katie and Max, listening to the throaty buzz of static on the line, staring at the green-striped cream wall-paper. Jude's mother answered, but he could hardly hear her. They interrupted each other, then simultaneously paused and waited for the other to speak, then she spoke and a cloud of static obscured her words. He heard *sorry*, he heard *tried to*, he heard *Jude*. He said: 'Is she, is she, is she there?' He heard *Stephen, she, speak to you, speak to you*.

He disconnected, staring at the vines climbing between the stripes, their tiny, veined leaves.

I listened in silence, my chin in my hand. Katie looked at me, waiting for a reaction.

'That would hurt.'

'He's got this hatchet, he chops up branches for the fireplace. When I came round the next day, he'd chopped up all the chairs in the house, they were in pieces on the floor.'

'And what did Max do?'

Katie paused, shrugged. 'He cleared out for a while. Couldn't really cope with it. Your brother . . .'

'What?'

'He'd slide away from anything like that.'

I took this in, added it to the Max jigsaw. It sounded right, he was good at withdrawing, bad at confrontations, at scenes, at any sort of emotional demands. Christmas was a trial, birthdays were a trial, withdrawal was not a trial, it was easy.

'So,' I said. 'Is it you and Stephen now?'

Katie smiled, like this was a foolish, inappropriate idea. The oddness of relationships. Katie and Stephen seemed like a good idea to me, an obvious one.

'No,' said Katie. 'No, no, no.'

'Why not?'

This time a pause, an outward movement of the lips.

'Stephen and women . . .' she began.

'Yes?'

She shook her head, perhaps feeling she'd already said too much. 'You're curious.'

'I'm nosy,' I corrected.

'But how about you?' she said. 'You fancy him?'

Now I paused, taken by surprise. 'Fancy him? What am I, twelve?'

Katie started grinning. 'You do, don't you?'

I shook my head firmly. 'He's too tidy. Something about him grates. He's too skinny, too serious. The only thing we have in common? We both like stories.'

Stephen didn't know why he was looking at his teaching notes. It was the beginning of the summer holidays, much too soon to be thinking about the classroom. Ways of incorporating maths into the topic of Romans and Greeks. Maybe the call from Griffin had got him thinking about work. His scribbled note said *Tuesday, 11.* An address in Manchester. A potential door opening, out of the classroom. He'd have to decide what he wanted. That question again: what was he going to do?

He was at the bottom of the stairs when he heard Gloria's voice.

'Something about him grates. He's too skinny, too

serious. The only thing we have in common? We both like stories.'

He hesitated. *She should talk about grating. And how can you be too serious?* He hesitated, detoured quietly to the kitchen, then came in a few minutes later with a mug of coffee. Gloria and Katie glanced at each other as he entered. The three letters were in Gloria's lap.

'Morning,' she said. 'How's the head?'

He sat down with his coffee. 'Terrible. Found any clues?'

Katie watched Stephen carefully. 'Gloria wants to visit Jude.'

'No.'

'I want to know what she knows,' said Gloria, reasonably. 'And you want to know why she's harassing you.'

'No way. Not a chance.' Stephen looked at the two women looking at him. 'I said *no*. Not going to happen.'

Ten minutes later they were on the road, Katie wishing them luck as she waved them off.

They climbed the long dual carriageway, winding up out of Halifax. Stephen's eye was caught as usual by the zeppelin-shaped balloon bobbing about ahead, advertising furniture. It tugged at its cable as if restless, wanting to escape the boxy warehouse it was attached to, wanting to try its luck in the big sky over the Calder valley.

'Tell me about her,' Gloria said. 'Go on, it might help.'

It was easier to answer her than not to, and once he started he found that words about Jude were stacked up inside him.

'We met at my parents' golden wedding. She was helping her mother, who runs a catering company. I talked to Jude instead of my parents' friends.'

The little white apron had caught his eye, the black

tights. 'Judy,' she'd said. 'Call me Jude.' It felt good to exchange a private smile with her when she was pouring champagne, a sliding look, like there was a connection between them that made them separate from everyone there. He had a suit on, which probably made him look more capable, more worldly than was strictly accurate. It was only a week later, when they went to see a film together, and had a long, talk-filled meal at a cheap Italian place, that he realised how strange she was. Still hard to see how her planet and his intersected, and how once they did, they managed to communicate.

'She was like an alien to me. Her background was quilted jackets and pearls. She said half her clothes used to be navy blue. But she said she'd escaped all that. That's what I admired, the way she'd decided to reinvent herself.'

'So you felt . . .?'

'I felt I loved her.' He thought a moment. 'I felt she'd help me to be myself.'

They were driving to Holmfirth, and now he found himself lamenting lost love as well as his lost friend. Max's death was beginning to feel like a brick through a large window, radiating cracks into every corner of the glass.

'I'm sorry,' said Gloria.

He glanced at her, didn't want to shrug, couldn't think what else to do. 'Yes,' he said.

Jude's. Fat, curly letters on the sign. As they pushed open the door, meat and cheese smells hit their nostrils, dense and peppery. A white-clad boy was unpeeling a slice of prosciutto from a machine; it hung from his fingers, delicate and clinging, like skin. Jude appeared behind him at the door of a dark back room, mid-sentence, and stopped. She stared at Stephen and Gloria for a moment.

'Stephen.'

She beckoned them through. They followed her, Stephen with his hand in his pocket, pinching the anonymous letters between finger and thumb. He took a straddling sort of step through the door, as if something was in his way. A physical awkwardness there, a nervousness.

Jude was standing behind a metal-topped table, folding filo over spiced vegetables. Buttering it, layering it into a neat triangle, putting it on a baking tray, starting on the next.

'Well,' she said, 'this is unexpected.'

Stephen watched her. She looked, with those cultured vowels, like a smart TV chef. She'd been taken aback to see him, but now she was finding her composure. He saw the way she'd put space between them, and given herself something to do with her hands. He thought of that day in the Registry Office. Joking at first, then getting nervous, then slowly realising that she wasn't going to turn up. A tight, hard ball had appeared in his chest, making it hard to breathe or speak. He hadn't thought there'd been a crash or a breakdown, or that Jude had been struck with a virus, or that the whole family had overslept. He'd known she'd changed her mind.

She looked at them over the samosas, hands floury, eyebrows slightly raised. With her pastry brush, she looked like an artist surprised by a film crew.

'Unexpected,' he said. He was trying to keep his tone neutral, but anger had arrived abruptly.

Jude looked at Gloria. Stephen didn't seem about to speak again, so she introduced herself.

'Gloria,' she said. 'Max's sister.'

'I'm sorry for your loss,' said Jude.

Stephen took out a letter, which felt greasy in his warm hand, and showed it to her, a touch of drama in the thrust of his arm. Jude peered at the wilting paper, screwing up her eyes as she read. Her glasses were beside her and he considered slotting them on to her face, but decided against it.

'So?' he said. The syllable seemed to quiver in the air between them.

Her lower lip, pink and glossy, jutted out a little. 'I'm sorry,' she said again, 'this is. . .?' That unruffled rhythm to her words, always controlled. 'Something that someone has sent you?'

She looked him in the eyes, then forked some more vegetables on to a page of filo.

'You're saying you don't know?'

'That's correct, Stephen, I'm saying I don't know what you're showing me. You surely don't think I sent it?'

He'd never been very good at reading her. Jude learnt about composure and poise from her mother, the same as she learnt about make-up and clothes. Confidence was in her blood. She stared at him, her brown eyes wide and challenging.

Gloria interrupted the silence. 'Do you think Stephen is truthful?'

She looked puzzled. 'Broadly speaking, yes, but he's quite wrong about this.' She looked at the first letter again. '*Your best friend's dead*,' she read aloud. 'Do you really believe I'd send you that? I wouldn't be so callous.'

Stephen sighed, knowing she was telling the truth.

'I wanted it to be you,' he said. 'I don't want this to be a mystery.'

Jude shook her head, said it for a third time: 'Sorry.'

Her arms were bare in the warm kitchen, revealing downy hair and a scatter of moles. Once, he'd counted the moles on her back. Little dabs of chocolate brown. He'd touched a fingertip to each. Twenty-two.

She opened the oven, releasing a gust of hot air which made him step back, reddening.

They sat on uncomfortable garden furniture in a yard outside the kitchen, waiting for Jude to join them. Gloria leant across to Stephen. 'Don't like her much,' she whispered. 'Posh cow. I'd say you're well out of it.'

Jude emerged before Stephen could answer. 'I have no notion why your brother did what he did,' she was speaking as she came out. 'I was appalled, and so sad,' she said, 'so sad that Max died that way.'

Stephen looked up quickly. 'We don't know what happened. He might have fallen.'

'Stephen . . .'

'He might have.'

This led to another pause. Words weren't coming easily, held up by the history between them. Stephen sipped cold water, tipped his face to catch the sun. He was still angry with her. He wanted her business to fail and he wanted her to catch some disfiguring disease. But he also felt, inside him, an emptiness, an inability to conjure speech.

She looked at him when he looked away. His face creased in the sunlight. 'I have a story for you,' she said. 'It's about me and Max.'

'You and Max?' It was a combination he found unlikely.

'I know something about him you don't.'

'Tell us,' said Gloria.

Jude nodded but hesitated, as if having second thoughts. Her fingers flickered for a moment in front of her mouth.

'A couple of months after our break-up,' she began, 'Max came round. I was puzzled, I wondered what this might be. Whether he was going to shout at me on your behalf, or convey a message. It was nothing like that. He looked at me, straight at me, touched the small of my back and said 'So Jude, how *are* you?'

Stephen stared as if she'd said something complicated.

She continued. 'In that serious voice he had. It was the touch, and the eyes and the tone, it was as if a switch flicked, as if an electric current was turned on.'

Stephen stared at her. 'You're telling me this?'

'You want to know, don't you? It wasn't, I wouldn't see it as a betrayal. Max loved you like a brother, but he was curious, he was curious about what happened between us.'

Curiosity, Stephen knew, was one of Max's qualities. Something in him, his stillness, seemed to respond to other people's traumas. He wasn't good at sympathy, or at picking up pieces, but he was interested in the mechanics of the drama. Sometimes a conversation with him was like one of those interviews you see on the news: *What happened? Why did you do that? And how did you feel, how did you feel?* He was like a scientist, using observation and inquiry, trying to understand something foreign to him.

'Go on,' said Gloria.

He'd looked straight into her eyes, used her name, and touched her. She'd laughed at the sudden effect this had, dissolving her poise. They'd sat in the kitchen and she'd told her side of the story: the growing doubt, the failure to say anything, the way she'd longed for an illness or even a death to release her.

Max had listened without judgement, asked questions without inflection. She'd loosened up, there's always something flattering in an attentive listener, especially if he's someone not close to you. It was late and her assistant closed up the shop and still they were talking. She told Max she'd won a prize for the second-best patisserie in West Yorkshire, and they messily feasted on left-over *mille-feuilles*. When she went back into the shop, behind the counter to empty the till, she felt his hands on her hips, and she straightened up against him, her back to him. He kissed her neck and moved his hands up her and around her, and when she turned to face him they slid down into the narrow space behind the counter.

Halfway through, something got jolted and fine icing sugar drifted down on top of them, dusting their bare skin, like a slow, harmless blizzard.

The story was over.

'He never told me,' said Stephen.

Jude nodded. 'But was I right to tell you? I thought you ought to know every side of him. And it was just something that happened. He wouldn't have hurt you for the world.'

'No? Why'd he kill himself, then? That hurt.'

She stared at him, started to speak, but he raised a finger. 'Don't,' he said. 'Just don't.'

Gloria stared at him too.

They drove several miles in silence. Max and Jude, Jude and Max. *I wouldn't see it as a betrayal.* How else could he see it?

'I'm glad you've accepted it was suicide.'

Gloria, intruding again, trying to sound casual. He didn't answer.

'So. Seen anyone since Jude?'

'Sure,' he said. 'Of course.'

'Anyone serious?'

'Leave me alone.'

He'd formulated a plan after Jude. He was going to stop needing and start being needed. He had a theory that this was the secret to a safe and productive life. If you need someone you're at their mercy, your well-being is in their hands. If they need you, you're in control. He'd told Max this, and Max had told him not to be so fucking stupid. (And was that before or after Max slept with Jude?)

A good stretch of road lay ahead. Stephen accelerated. Now here he was with Max's sister, on her mission to find out why Max had died. He refused to be analysed. He would say nothing.

He said, 'I wish Jude had sent the letters.'

He was surprised to hear his own voice. The line between thinking and speaking seemed to have blurred.

'I know. You told her that.'

He was irritated with Gloria for knowing, for replying, for asking personal questions, for needling him, for being there at all.

'I want to uncover some facts.' He spoke quickly, angrily, as if it was something he'd explained several times before. 'I want to investigate them, and then point a finger and say: *You're behind this*. I want to be able to say: *This is why what happened, happened*. Instead it turns out I didn't even know him, didn't even know my best friend.'

'He made himself difficult to know. That's why we're doing this, isn't it? We're trying to know Max.'

They drove on, and now Max was a presence in the seat behind them; intractable and silent.

Story of a Spider

I LIKE TO PILFER. I like the word. I imagine a hand slipping between sheets of paper on a desk, or between layers of clothing. Stephen was downstairs, banging about in the kitchen, I was in his room, wondering if he was bad-tempered and unfriendly because of Jude, because of me, or because he'd finally acknowledged that Max had killed himself. Perhaps he felt responsible for Max's death. Perhaps he'd somehow failed Max. I imagined Max needing to talk, Stephen being too busy; or the two of them having an argument, Stephen coming out with some casual but devastating criticism; or Stephen losing something, a cheque or a vital letter, something that would have led Max on to a new, more promising stage in his life. So many ways a friend can let you down.

He was still downstairs. I'd told him I was going to rest for a while, and I was genuinely tired; Hong Kong time still confusing me, grief wearing me out, but I'd paused outside his door and impulsively slipped in. On Saturday morning I'd read his letters, now I wanted to explore further.

Books and CDs in alphabetical order, bed neatly made, carpet recently hoovered. *OK*, I thought, *I know who you are*. Then I opened some drawers. Shirts, T-shirts, underwear and socks stuffed in together. In the third drawer, underneath the clothes, I found his Jude archive. Letters and photographs, a ticket for Glastonbury, a restaurant receipt. It might have been a romantic collection, but the letters were covered with creases, and the photographs were dog-eared and Sellotaped. It looked as if he'd started to destroy all evidence of Jude, then repaired it, then assaulted it all again. Hard to know what to make of Stephen. Hard to know what he made of himself.

As I sat at his desk, I heard movement downstairs. He'd left the kitchen. I should get out of his room, should never have entered it in the first place. It was another unplanned, unwise decision, leaving me feeling I wasn't in control of myself. Just another few moments. I opened a photograph album I'd found, listening, hoping he'd go into the sitting room. The album didn't contain photographs. On each page there was a twisted bouquet of ageing hair trapped beneath clear plastic film. He was on the stairs, he was going to find me, but I couldn't help staring at the hair-album. Ignoring his approaching footsteps, I opened the desk drawer. It contained twelve teeth.

He was on the landing. I heard him pause, and I froze, tried to summon a plausible excuse.

But he walked past his bedroom, to the bathroom. Closing the album, closing the desk drawer, I felt like a forensic investigator, piecing together the evidence of an old, ghastly crime.

The bathroom door shut, and I let out a long breath I hadn't realised I'd been holding. I slipped out of his room, and into mine. Feeling jittery and weary at the same time. I needed to lie down, needed to stay still for a while. I dropped on to my bed. Sleep was unlikely, but I could close my eyes at least, just to rest, just to try to relax.

I dreamt Max was running towards me, and I was glad. He was running out of darkness and it was dark behind me, but I stood in an angle of light. Opened my arms. The thought of embracing him was an intense pleasure, but something was wrong, he was running towards me but he wasn't slowing down. I moved, my face pleading, but he was already passing, I couldn't even lay a finger on him and then he was gone, running away, into the darkness behind me.

After that there was something uneven but vivid about Stephen in Max's bedroom, my room, with his hatchet, chopping up furniture. He stared at me as I sat up, and grinned. 'Don't worry,' he said, 'I just want your teeth.'

I woke sweating and panting, sat up, and Stephen was there, by the bed, staring at me, his hands behind his back. What was he holding? Was I still dreaming?

'What? What do you want?'

He took a step back, revealed empty hands. 'Sorry, I didn't know you were asleep.'

'What time is it?'

'Five. In the evening.'

'Jet lag,' I sighed. I looked at him, focusing slowly. 'Jet lag,' I repeated.

We were in the sitting room again, short of words again, like an old married couple who have gradually, over years, withdrawn their intimacy from each other. Me on the blue sofa, him on the blue armchair, sitting in the pale sunlight falling through the window. Still tired, but no longer jittery, I looked into the large glass of wine I was holding, then glanced up as Stephen did. He looked at me, really looked, meeting my eyes, perhaps thinking of that moment between Max and Jude, his almost-wife. No switch was flicked, no electric current was turned on, but I managed a smile anyway. Both of us needed some comfort.

'You're still angry with her, aren't you?'

'I think I might always be. For a while afterwards I wasn't nice to be with.'

'But now?'

'Now I'm great to be with.'

My smile widened. 'Humour.'

Stephen leant forward abruptly, encouraged.

'I've got a story about Jude,' he said. 'Want to hear it?'

'Of course.' I took a deep swallow of wine, hoping this wouldn't involve some petty character assassination.

'It's about when she lost her virginity. The whole thing was recorded. She told me—her words— that there was an unfortunate accident involving touch controls and flailing toes. And then her mother set the tape going when she was dusting. So she's standing there, in her little girl's room, and she's suddenly hearing the whole event, the grunts and groans, the shouts, everything.'

'Shouts?'

'Apparently. And Jude kept the tape. This is the weird part. She kept the tape, and sometimes she liked to play it when we made love.'

I stared at him. He was grinning, pleased with my reaction. 'And you know why she told us about her and Max, don't you?' I said. 'Because she was scoring points. I've got two words for you, Stephen: lucky escape.'

Something happened. In spite of the Jude archive, and hair and teeth, and that dream, and him standing there, watching me, something happened. The Jude story got us started. The awkwardness dissolved, the effort dissolved, and for the first time we were unguarded with each other. We were just two people drinking wine and talking. I was too sleepy to make an effort, disorientated by my nap; he seemed a little dazed by the news he'd received from Jude. We were like a couple of outpatients, Max's death like an illness we had in common. Of course the archive, the hair and the teeth, the dream and him standing there with his hands hidden were all still in my mind, like a radio playing quietly in another room.

'All right,' I said. 'Now I know Max shagged the woman who jilted you, he liked that dumb club, he once snapped a cat's tail in two, he kept a bayonet under his pillow. And some mystery person knows him well enough to send you strange letters about him.'

'You're doing pretty well.'

'It's just fragments, it's pieces of Max, I want more. Like why did he do it? Why did he do it at that particular time? Was there an incident? Something that happened?'

Stephen was shaking his head. 'My sense,' he said, 'is Max was carrying something heavy for a long time, and he was tired, he was weary, so finally he stopped carrying it.'

A pause, while we considered that. It had the flavour to me of a formula of words he'd settled for. But I didn't want to settle for anything, I wanted to question, to bat ideas back and forth, to arrive at a conclusion.

'Who's sending the letters?'

'No idea.'

'Come on, Stephen, suspects. If not Jude, who?'

'I don't know, I don't know.'

'Well, what else can you tell me about my brother?'

We were handling Max's wooden box, passing it back and forth, upending it, shaking it, looking for a catch, a keyhole, a hinge. There seemed to be no way into it. I could imagine Max grinning as he designed it, pleased at the thought of frustrating his friends. He was playing a game with us, manipulating us.

'Maybe we should break it open,' said Stephen.

'I know,' I said. 'We should.' I was holding it as I spoke, my fingers wrapped protectively around it. 'But we can't. Not yet, anyway.'

I handed it back to Stephen, and he nodded. He put it on the floor and it drew our eyes like a suspect package, liable to explode. He started to tell me about Max.

'His work was everything, but he never believed praise, and when he got criticism he thought they'd seen through him.'

'You saw him at work?'

'His work was everything, but he liked not working. I'd arrive and he'd have this torch in his hand, oxy–acety-lene, and there'd be this spindly structure, like Meccano, only with pulleys and maybe, somewhere inside it, from a certain angle, a face. But he'd put down the torch when I came in, and want to do something else.'

I drew slowly and deeply on my cigarette. Since those days in the garage under the house, I hadn't seen Max at work. I'd missed a major part of his life.

'But he had a studio?' I said.

'Didn't like it. Said the light was better in his room. He didn't talk about it in terms of brightness, he talked about its weight. He said the light in his studio was heavy.'

'Heavy light?'

'That's what he said.'

'And what else?'

Stephen thought for a moment. I could see this was the sort of conversation he liked. That odd, unplanned but hoped–for thing, where one person picks up another's cue, half smiles and nods keeping up an easy momentum. I liked it too. I could hear the music of it, the easy give and take of it, verses and refrains. Max this, Max that, stories on stories.

'He was more confident physically than verbally.'

'And you're the opposite, aren't you?'

Stephen looked surprised, considered this. 'I'm quite good at acting confident,' he said.

'Which is very like being confident.'

He shrugged. I thought of what Katie had said. *You fancy him?* I couldn't fancy a man who shrugged as much as Stephen.

'Max was shy,' I said. 'It's a family problem.'

Stephen smiled, I didn't. He continued.

'Max told me he'd like to be better with people, he could see it was a useful skill. He said he became earnest when he should be light, he had no knack for small talk, his efforts at warmth sounded patronising.'

I felt a little discomfort returning. Stephen was looking at his fingernails and our unprecedented light mood was in danger of vanishing.

It was time for me to tell a story.

'Know how Max got his name?' I said.

Stephen perked up at this, waited. So I told him.

Stella always said she found Max under a bush, and she was telling the truth. No way was she going to let a little thing like nine months of pregnancy hold her up. Harry was saying, 'Stop, just for God's sake stop, and sit down,' but Stella brushed him out of the way. 'I'm having a walk this afternoon, I'm going to the cinema, you can come if you want.' But Harry had to go to work. 'So what if the baby was due last week?' Stella said. 'It'll be two weeks late and they'll induce. Nothing's ever happened to me on time.' This was Stella on good form, sure of herself, and funny, and brooking no argument. Maybe she was reckless too, maybe her hormones were slapping her around a bit.

Max surprised her, of course. She had him under a bush in the park that evening, screaming and swearing at the sky. She sent someone to call an ambulance, and he did as he was told. The police later said that, judging by his record, he'd probably been intending to mug her. That was Stella, though. She had this air of authority, always. The paramedics arrived in time to assist at the birth.

And the name of the mugger, the putative mugger, was Max.

'Good story,' Stephen said. 'Your mother sounds a strong personality.'

'Max never talked about her?'

'No. I'd tell him stories about my family, he'd keep quiet about his.'

'Stella is a good story, but it doesn't end well.'

Stephen said nothing, unsure what to do with this statement. When it was clear I wasn't going to say any more, he changed the subject.

'Max once told me he liked his name,' he said. 'One short, punchy syllable. He said that you had to make your mouth into a kiss to say it.'

And then we were silently saying *Max*, making air-kisses at each other. Stephen sitting there, thin and pale and pushing his face into unusual shapes, his hairy hands laid in his lap, his wrinkly eyes looking at my mouth. He was not particularly comfortable in his skin, and his relaxed mood was fragile, but for now, at this moment, I felt content in his company. Because I was sitting there too, saying *Max* with my lips thrust out towards Stephen, catching sight of myself and feeling surprised. Recognising a little current of sex between us, and wondering if it would come to anything. I'm in a strange house, half-drunk, blowing kisses at a strange man, thousands of miles from everything I'm familiar with. But content, because maybe I need a little strangeness and disruption in my life, maybe I've withdrawn too much, like my brother, like my brother.

A spider is crucial here. Thanks to a spider, I slept with Stephen. That's how life is: you think you have a will and a purpose, you think with detours and mistakes you're finding your own way through. You're not though. A spider, the weather, the flow of traffic, will choose for you who you meet, how you act, whether you live or die.

Midnight. God knows what time my body thought it was, but I was ready for bed. I got in, lay down, and as I reached for the light I became aware of movement somewhere at the edge of my vision, just beyond the eyelid. My head tilted, and there it was above me, big as a baby's splayed hand, crawling on the ceiling. Its fat stomach slung in the cradle of its skinny legs. It was scuttling, repulsively delicate, and it was in trouble. I was frozen beneath it, hand still stretched out towards the light, and it was in trouble.

As I watched it dropped, fell inches through clear air towards me, then caught itself. My body jerked but otherwise I didn't move, watched it haul itself slowly back up its lifeline. I thought I'd wait till it was back on the ceiling, then execute some sort of slithering manoeuvre to get myself out from underneath it while keeping my eyes at all times fixed on it. That was my plan, it was an entirely plausible plan, but useless, because as I watched the spider dropped a second time, failed to catch itself and fell directly into my bed.

I yelled something incomprehensible, levitated off my mattress, shot out of my room and arrived in Stephen's, all in the same sliver of a second.

After standing there at the end of his bed, panting, trying to get the words out, looking presumably like I'd lost my mind, I conveyed what had happened.

He said, 'Oh, you're fucking joking. In the bed? Are

you sure? I'm not going in there, I don't even feel safe here.'

Him in bed, me standing there in my T-shirt. Staring at each other. This was a moment we hadn't expected to arrive at. There was some negotiation, talk of the sofa downstairs, a sleeping bag in a cupboard somewhere, and then I sneezed and after a few more moments we were in bed together.

He turned towards me and I turned towards him. There was still about a foot between us. Me breathless, him adjusting.

'Some day,' he said.

We stared at each other, and then his hand moved slowly to my hair, which was dirty, and stroked it. I touched his face, more exploratory than sexual, as if feeling for something there that I hadn't been able to find by looking. Did I want this? I'd thought about it in the club. It had been there between us all evening. I could feel the shape of my lips. My skin felt taut and fragile, like kite material. When I'd dreamt we were digging together, we'd both been naked, our fingers mingling in the dry earth. Did I want him on me? His weight pressing on me, urgent and pleased and angry?

We were still staring at each other. A long, dangling moment. I said, without premeditation, 'Max loved you like a brother. According to Jude.'

He nodded. 'Makes us almost related.'

Silence. And still a foot of creased sheet between us.

His hand withdrew. So did mine. He said, 'Does this feel right?'

I didn't answer. I said good night, and we turned our backs to each other. So we slept together, that's all.

Monday

Close

STEPHEN WOKE, OPENED his eyes, and saw the bedside table, the curtains. Had he dreamt it? And if he hadn't, was she still there? He wished he'd had sex with her. She was irritating, but she had a nice body and big eyes, he could imagine his face above hers, them staring at each other, gasping, that anger they each seemed to harbour perhaps making it better. He was wide awake quickly, he had an erection and he was in the midst of a discussion with himself.

When she'd mentioned Max—suddenly he'd been there in the room with them, suddenly there was nothing sexual between them.

He lay still, looking at his clock radio, trying and failing to hear her breathing. 7:34. Was she even there any more? He thought there was a weight on the other side of the bed, a falling away of the mattress, but he wasn't sure. He inched himself back towards the middle of the bed, hoping to feel her presence as if by accident. He remembered mornings with Rachel, waking up with her hands on him, wordless sex before the day or even consciousness had intervened. If Gloria was there, how would she feel about being woken with a kiss? What had she been wearing? Had she been wearing anything?

She spoke. 'Wish I'd never left the country.'

For a moment he thought she was talking in her sleep.

'If I'd loved Max more, perhaps I'd have stayed in England, and he'd have stayed alive.'

She seemed to think they were in the middle of a conversation over coffee in the kitchen.

'I wish somehow I could have got between him and the world.'

Stephen stopped his inching, said nothing.

'Are you awake?' she whispered. 'I thought you moved.'

They were lying back to back, and his bum was just grazing hers. Skin on skin. 'Yeah, I'm awake.'

'What do you think?'

'About you staying in England? I think that's bollocks.'

He swung his legs out of bed and sat up. He hadn't thought about it, it was just an irritable displacement of energy, but now he had to pretend he had a purpose.

'Coffee?'

'Thanks.'

His boxer shorts were on the floor near the door. He started to shuffle over the duvet, then felt stupid. He stood up, crossed the room, picked them up and went out.

Coffee in bed involved them both sitting up in T-shirts, that chaste foot apart again, their eyes on parallel lines gazing at the opposite wall. She clutched her mug as if her hands were cold, he balanced his on his raised knee. He was wondering what would happen if he turned to her and kissed her now. The moment was receding, had been receding ever since she mentioned Max last night. It was still there, quite a reasonable possibility, when he'd first woken up, but it felt more remote now, and soon it would be out of sight. Should he turn to her and kiss her? He judged that speech might serve him better than silence.

'No post yet.'

She stared at him, suddenly alert. 'Think there'll be another letter?'

He'd said the wrong thing, changed the mood. It was intriguing, of course, but was it really all she cared about at this moment? He shrugged, and they were quiet again. He'd thought he was beyond this awkward, adolescent behaviour. Apparently not, apparently this clumsy teenager had been lurking inside him all along. Gloria was staring at the crenellations of duvet over their feet. They were returning to normality. Now, if ever, was the time to act. Was there any discreet, adult way to cross that foot of sheet between them? He didn't want to lunge, or fall towards her. He took a breath, started to slowly turn.

I woke, opened my eyes, and saw a desk, Stephen's desk. I was in his room, in his bed, with him. I had a head ache, and I was thirsty. Every morning I'd been here, I'd woken up feeling terrible. I was thinking I should slip out of his bed before he woke up. Then he stirred. Maybe it was too late. What to do? I'd seriously considered sex last night, but now, in the grey morning, all I wanted was some water, a fag, more sleep. His duvet smelt suspect. He probably wasn't even scared of spiders.

I'd dreamt of Max again. (Stephen moved again.) We were on the beach in Scarborough, building a sandcastle. (Definitely a deliberate movement.) We were going for something elaborate and imposing, in spite of the tide approaching, creeping up the beach towards us. Our last day together. (Stephen's bum touched mine.) I tried to imagine a different reality, one in which Stephen and I shared a bed, while Max lay asleep in his room next door.

I spoke. 'Wish I'd never left the country.'

He was still. 'If I'd loved Max more perhaps I'd have stayed in England, and he'd have stayed alive.'

No answer and no movement. Nothing happening except me lying there looking at the desk, saying intimate things into the silence.

'I wish somehow I could have got between him and the world.'

Still no answer. I asked him if he was awake.

'Yeah, I'm awake.'

That was the tone of a man who wanted to talk about sex, not dead friends. I asked him for his opinion, he didn't have one, and he marched off to make coffee.

I wondered if Max had imagined a scene like this, had thought beyond his own death at all. Perhaps not, perhaps a man killing himself would find it impossible to look into the future. He clearly hadn't considered the feelings of the train driver. If he had, he might have found a quiet place to do it, a hotel room perhaps, where he was unlikely to scare anybody.

Stephen shouldered the door open, carrying his two coffees. Got back into bed without a word. A bad atmosphere was hanging in the air, as if we'd had an argument about sex, conducted through small movements and irrelevant comments. I sipped my coffee.

'No post yet.'

Good. This was what I wanted to be talking about.

'Think there'll be another letter?'

He just shrugged. Silence again. He shifted, restless. If sex was on his mind, he was expressing it entirely through irritability. I was tempted to tell him to grow up, then walk out, but it would be a shame to waste the progress we'd made. If sex was on his mind, I needed to distract him. Time perhaps to offer him another story.

He was turning towards me, perhaps about to speak. I got in first.

'Want to hear some more about Stella?' I said.

He hesitated. He straightened, turned away, sighed.
'Sure. Sure, go ahead.'
So I told him.

Stella had odd habits, eccentric episodes. She once spent all night watching television with the sound turned down. She once spent a full day speaking an entirely made-up language. After Gloria left home, things got worse. A couple of weeks after she'd moved out, Gloria received a call from Max. Could she come? Could she come immediately?

Gloria went round, and Max let her in. He didn't say anything, he just opened the door and walked back to the sitting room. She entered. There was something wrong with the phone in the hall. It was off the hook, the plastic was fractured in the cradle, and there was a deep untidy crater in the old-fashioned round dial. As Gloria fingered it, she found that its cord had been cut. She went into the sitting room and found Max and her mother cross-legged on the floor there. Her mother humming. Most of the glass had been knocked out of the television, the radio had been attacked too, and the neat CD system they'd bought her last Christmas was pockmarked with hammer blows. Blood was dripping from Stella's hand.

Gloria felt an almost exhilarating surge of panic. Max was silently sitting there, next to Stella. Had they both lost it? Perhaps they'd lured her here in order to turn on her. She started to speak, she was just going to say her brother's name, but Stella looked up with a finger to her lips. Max looked up too. He caught her eye, there was a flicker of his mouth, not quite a smile but an acknowledgement, and he winked. What could Gloria do? She sat down with her mother and her brother. The three of them on the floor, cross-legged and quiet, while the rest of the world went about its loud business, all around them.

'The door locked behind me when I went in, and Mum had hidden the key. We had to break a window to get out.'

Stephen didn't speak, not sure what to say.

'Max never told you that story?'

'Never breathed a word.'

Stephen wondered about this. It was another layer Max had kept hidden, careful as a double agent trying to blend in to hostile surroundings.

Gloria half-smiled, seeming to read Stephen's mind. 'Max and I have our mother's social skills.'

'No. Don't say that, it's not true.'

She got out of bed at last. 'Anyway, just thought you should have the whole story.'

He nodded. 'Thank you.'

'Or another piece towards it.'

He watched her go, her T-shirt not quite covering her naked bum, and he tried to decide if she'd sensed his movement towards her, and told the story simply to forestall him. Odd, how these most painful fragments tumble out of their dark places. She'd gone and he was alone again. He placed his hand palm down on the space where she'd been sitting, feeling the vanishing warmth.

About Rachel

S TEPHEN HADN'T READ a newspaper since Max
died. Whatever was going on in the world was unim-
portant, didn't measure up to what was going on in his
life. Unless there'd been a headline, *Max Rumat Kills
Himself*, and a few columns devoted to the story, some
features on the inside pages, an obituary, photographs,
he simply couldn't muster the interest. But when Gloria
came into the kitchen, he was guiding cornflakes to his
mouth while reading an article about the state of British
farming with complete conviction. He looked up at
her, said, 'Help yourself', with a wave at the cereal, and
returned to the industrialisation of agriculture. He listened to Gloria's movements behind him and wondered
if he'd overdone it—he was aiming for casual, but was
aware he might be bordering on churlish.

'No sign of the spider,' she said.

'You checked the bed?'

'On it, in it, under it.'

She was holding something. Max's wooden brick.
She sat down and positioned it on end, on the table. He
looked at it, and at her, but she had a spoon in her mouth
now so her expression was unclear. He wasn't sure if the
brick was intended as a conversational opening, a challenge, or if it was just an innocent impulse. She might
be bad tempered. If so, was it in response to him reading
the paper, was it something to do with sharing a bed,

was she regretting telling him about her mother, or did it predate all those things? His relationships with women were always flawed, but he wasn't aware of any other in his life which was so hedged by questions and doubt.

Max's brick sat at the apex of their triangle. It was more than a symbol, it was a presence, it was Max again, sitting there as he'd sat in the back of the car on the way back from Jude's, as he'd appeared in the bedroom last night, mutely observing them floundering in his absence. He'd like being a ghost; he'd be intrigued, he'd sit forward watching Stephen and Gloria with keen interest, even amusement.

'I may leave,' she said.

'Back to Hong Kong?'

'No, I might visit somewhere that was important to us. To Max and me. I had a dream last night.'

She was going to tell him about the day she found the hermit crab's shell, about the beach, the sandcastle, the approaching tide, but she was interrupted. The rattle of the letter box, the splash of the post. A beat, an amplified moment, as if one of them had said something harsh, involving a degree of recoil and surprise. Then Stephen was on his feet. Perhaps there'd be no letter, perhaps there'd be silence in the one-way conversation. He wasn't sure which he'd prefer.

He opened the box clinging to the back of the front door, fished out the envelopes, sorted through them (junk, a bill, a postcard), and instantly recognised the typeface. Bringing it back to the kitchen, he separated the letter from the others, held it in a different hand, slightly away from his body, like a man carrying a glass of hot water, full to the brim and liable to spill.

Funny, death.
How it makes you realise
you didn't know Max as well as
you'd have liked,
or as well as you should have.
The experiences that defined him,
what preoccupied him,
his favourite places.
Want to know more about him?
Ask Rachel.

'The experiences that defined him.' Stephen read the words aloud, looked at Gloria. 'Is that about your mother? Is it someone who knows him that well?'

'Don't know,' said Gloria, 'but I have a question. You went all quiet when it came up before: who's Rachel?'

The letter was flattened on the table between them, along with the other three, and the cruel sketch of Rachel they'd found in Max's room. His box standing over the papers like a miniature version of the monolith from 2001.

'Rachel's another ex. You think he slept with her too?'

'We better ask her.'

Stephen picked up Max's box. Look at it another way, it was like a miniature cabinet, but without a door. He understood Gloria's reluctance to break it, he shared it, but at the same time he felt like throwing it on to the floor, stamping on it till it cracked open, revealed its secrets, making these investigations unnecessary. He wasn't sure he could cope with much more picking at the loose ends of his life.

Karen brings the drinks to Simon's table and sits down.
KAREN: So, who's Rose?

SIMON: What?

KAREN: I know who she is, but to you, who is she? Is she important? The love of your life?

SIMON: Karen.

KAREN: Say I'm Rose. I'm Rose. You love me?

SIMON: I don't really get love.

KAREN: That's a 'No' then.

SIMON: Can't I just like her? I like her a lot, I like spending time with her, I like to smell her hair when she's sleeping, I have no problem with Rose.

KAREN: Still a 'No'.

SIMON: Does it matter?

KAREN: Depends. Maybe you're not in love. Fair enough. But maybe you are in love and you can't admit it, because you have a problem with women.

SIMON: OK. Which is it? Do I have a problem, or am I not in love?

KAREN: My opinion? I don't know how you feel about Rose, but you definitely have a problem.

Karen laughs at him and takes a drink.

In the car, Gloria said, 'So, tell me about Rachel.'

Stephen shook his head. 'Weren't those your exact words about Jude? What are you, my biographer?'

But he told her. The self-absorption, the wine in the face, the curls and the lipstick and the teeth.

Gloria listened without comment. It didn't take him long to summarise Rachel, and the relationship. When he'd finished, she said, 'How did you feel about her?'

He glanced at her. 'Didn't I just say?'

'No.'

She was disconcerting, Gloria. He didn't know whether she set out to disconcert, but it was the effect she had.

How had he felt about Rachel? Difficult to peel away the rancour. He'd been new at the school, hopeful but apprehensive. In the staff room he'd made a sarcastic remark to someone, which was meant to show that he was friendly and had a sense of humour. It resulted in a silence, a perceptible cooling of the atmosphere. It was Rachel who laughed, said something which defused his comment, even implied its harmlessness. They'd had a drink after work, he'd thanked her, she'd said it was good to see some talent on the teaching staff, so he'd asked her if she was busy that Friday night.

'Grateful,' he said. 'I felt grateful to her. And I fancied her, of course. But something went wrong.'

'What went wrong?'

He didn't answer.

'What's the longest you've been with a woman, Stephen?'

He still didn't answer. Then he did. 'Fuck off,' he said.

She taught him the number plate game and quickly spotted *Arachnid Fear Erupts*. Then *Rachel Tells All*. Stephen drove on silently, along the road to Todmorden. He didn't seem to be playing, seemed to be dwelling still on their previous exchange. Gloria glanced at him, he watched the road until some minutes later when he noticed a number plate on a car in front. He tried to keep his tone flat, neither bitter nor regretful.

'Sex Narrowly Avoided,' he said.

'That's not a headline.'

He didn't answer.

It was only as they approached Rachel's front door that he let himself wonder what kind of reception they'd get.

He should have phoned, but she might have refused to see them. '*Friendly*,' she'd sneered at him, four days earlier. They were through the gate and approaching the door and he couldn't even slow down now, couldn't plan some lines or arrange his face because Gloria was beside him and he didn't want to look stupid, or feeble, so he just walked up to the door, just walked up and knocked.

No response for a few seconds. *Perhaps she's out?* Then he heard her approaching, that hope shrivelled, and the door swung open. She looked at him, glanced at Gloria, then back at him. What she said shocked him.

'I'm glad you came.'

In that slice of time while he'd heard her approaching, Stephen had managed to prepare his first words. They'd been intended to deflect hostility, but they'd still do.

'This is Max's sister, Gloria. She wants to meet people who knew him.'

Rachel held out her hand and Gloria shook it. It made Stephen wonder again why he hadn't kissed or shaken hands with Gloria when he first met her, and had barely touched her since. Still that awkward, unbridged distance between them.

'I didn't know him,' Rachel was saying. 'I hardly knew him at all.' She seemed to notice suddenly that they were still on the doorstep. 'But come in.'

They spoke about traffic and weather as she brought in mugs of tea. Her sitting room was small, but full of light. Yellow walls, a striped rug on the floorboards, a tall green plant reaching out from the corner. He'd felt welcomed when he first walked in, welcomed by the room itself, the warm and well-lit space. It had been an exciting time: a new job, a new girlfriend. It was a bright autumn day and they'd made love on the rug in a slab of sunshine, laughing at their own eagerness, their good fortune.

She sat, looked at him, sighed. 'Thursday, I was in a foul mood. I realised afterwards it was the day before the funeral. I'm sorry.'

'I really do wish we could be friends.'

Abruptly, there was ice in her voice. 'I expect you do.'

'God,' said Gloria. 'There was some feeling in that.'

And then weirdly, horribly, the two women were talking about him. Rachel said he was constipated, emotionally, Gloria said she'd noticed; Gloria described his expression when she gate-crashed the funeral, Rachel recalled throwing the wine in his face. They were both laughing.

Stephen sat back, and then after a moment leant forward. 'OK,' he said, 'let's do this.' And he told Rachel she was self-obsessed, told Gloria she was arrogant and rude and everything she said seemed to have an accusation wrapped up inside it. Gloria said that was guilt talking, but what did he expect, when she read letters that said he wasn't telling the truth and he knew why Max had killed himself, and by the way, why was he was so distant and unfriendly; Rachel said she wasn't self-obsessed, she was just trying to get him to talk about feelings; Stephen asked Gloria was she calling him a liar, and said to Rachel he was perfectly capable of talking about feelings, thanks very much. Gloria turned to Rachel, 'Did you know about his hair collection, and the teeth? Is that creepy or what?' Rachel ignored her, glaring at Stephen, 'You think you understand feelings? You didn't even notice I loved you.'

And then there was some silence. All three of them breathing heavily, like they'd been exercising, and overdoing it, unused to such a strenuous work-out.

One minute I'm agonising about things not being said, the next it's all spilled out like a huge stain on the rug between us, and we'd like to ignore it but we can't take our eyes off it. If I was more practised at getting to know people I'd probably find a more elegant way to do it, involving a process of gradual warming to someone, more of that musical conversation. Meanwhile, I'll have to settle for silence, faulty phones, deceptions, raised voices and sudden, alarming disclosures. I sit there, wondering if I should just sidle out, but not wanting to, wanting to stay and watch. Stephen looks like she's slapped him hard in the face, or thrown wine at him again; Rachel's embarrassed, aware of the melodrama, but unable at this point to retract. Maybe it's down to me to mediate.

Rachel turns to me before I can speak. 'They're his grandmother's teeth.'

Stephen: 'She'd kept them. Then I kept them. Something of hers, that's all. A memento.'

I nodded, like this made perfect sense. 'And the hair?'

'When I was fourteen, me and my girlfriend exchanged locks of hair. It got into a habit. What were you doing in my room?'

'Wait a minute. You're saying you always collect hair from your girlfriends?'

'You were in my room, weren't you? Looking through my stuff.'

I wondered if he'd understand if I said I liked to pilfer. 'I think you're evading the issue,' I told him, looking at Rachel.

A little more silence. There were a few issues swirling around now for us all to digest, and perhaps evade. For the first time I could see why people contemplated threesomes. Not so much for the sex, more for the sheer energy liable to be generated.

Stephen took a deep breath. 'This is the issue.' He handed Rachel the letters.

We watched as she read them. That same mix of con-
centration and puzzlement we'd seen in Jude. Was there
something else, though? A stillness about her, as if she was
controlling her reaction. A movement of her lips, as if she
was considering saying something. On the other hand,
given the words that had just been said, maybe she was
still recovering from that exchange. Impossible to know
what was going on behind her face. Telepathy would
have been useful.

She handed them back. 'Whoever it is,' she said, 'seems
to know you pretty well.'

Stephen accepted the letters. 'Obviously you didn't . . .
I have to ask . . . you didn't write them?'

She looked at him. 'Obviously not.'

Another dead end. I suddenly lost interest in Stephen's
failed relationships. 'But what can you tell us about Max?'

Rachel seemed to consider a moment, then spoke. 'I
went round once, to his place.' A nod towards Stephen.
'After he'd dumped me.'

Stephen looked surprised. 'You did?'

'Max was supposed to tell you.'

'Wait a minute,' said Stephen. 'Did you sleep with
him?'

She looked towards me, embarrassed. 'Tell you the
truth, I didn't even like him.'

In the sunshine in the yellow room in the aftermath
of all the shouting, I tried and failed to smile at her. It
felt more like a quiver of my lips, like I was trying not
to reveal some wayward emotion. I took Stephen's role.

'Go on,' I said.

Max had something wrong with his throat. He was whispering, but he beckoned Rachel in. He poured some
wine and they sat in the window in the front room. She'd

assumed she was waiting for Stephen, but Max breathed something about him being away for the day.

'Then why am I still here?' she asked.

He raised his eyebrows, did a little you-tell-me motion with his hands. She found it irritating, and it must have showed on her face because his manner quickly changed, he apologised and asked if there was anything she'd like him to tell Stephen. There was a lot Rachel wanted to say, but she hadn't planned on it going through an intermediary. While she was considering a pithy message for him, Max produced a sketch pad from somewhere, and started drawing her. He studied her, drew a line, smiled when she looked at him and told her she had an unusually mobile face.

Rachel tolerated this for a minute, then said, 'Do you find this approach works very often?'

She felt the weight of his attention shift. He still made marks on the paper, but he was no longer trying to make a connection. He started telling her some story about a family trip to Scarborough: a sandcastle, a view, messages in bottles thrown out to sea. She didn't know what he was on about or why he was telling her; his thinking seemed to be a little disorganised.

She left Max sitting there with his unfinished sketch and his unfinished story, and a message for Stephen to ring her. It was the Easter holidays, and Stephen's silence for the three weeks that followed helped her to hate him.

So easy for friends to let you down. I thought of the spiteful caricature of Rachel I'd found. I thought of her waiting to hear from Stephen, who never knew she'd visited.

'Sorry,' said Rachel. 'It's not what you want to hear about your brother, but he was a jerk that day.'

I'd had a lot of momentum when I'd got off the plane on Friday, it had kept me going over a busy weekend, but now it was Monday lunch time, I was hearing about a side of my brother I didn't like, and I was weary.

I looked at Stephen. 'Can we go home?'

Some awkwardness in the hall, Stephen repeating that he didn't know Rachel had come to see him, Rachel shrugging like it didn't make much difference. 'But we have to talk,' she said. 'We have to talk soon.' And then we were gone.

As soon as the front door shut behind us I asked Stephen what he thought that meant, *We have to talk*. He said he thought it was personal. I asked him if he thought she was telling the truth. He looked surprised. 'Of course.' I didn't pursue it. Instead, as we drove away, I told Stephen my theory about how life is balanced, like plates spinning on sticks. You can adapt to any number of imperfections—a wine stain on your best dress, a broken wrist, sleeping with the wrong bloke—until death drops into your life and it's too big. Everything just stops.

'My life has stopped,' I said, 'and I don't know how to start it again.'

Stephen sighed. 'We can't get over him while these letters are arriving.'

I said nothing. I didn't mean my life stopped when Max died, I meant it stopped when Stella died and I ran away to Hong Kong, but I said nothing about that. I didn't like *get over him*, but I said nothing about that either, because Stephen, I now realised, had been quietly getting angry. He'd been angry after he saw Jude, and he was angry now, having seen Rachel. I remembered Katie's unfinished sentence, trailing off, *Stephen and women . . .*

'I'm not going to let these letters rule my life for the next God knows how long. I'm not going to let them force me to see people I don't want to see, talk to people I don't want to talk to. Next one that comes, I'm throwing it away. I'm throwing it away without opening it. These can go now.'

We were at the mini-roundabout, turning towards Hebden, a big Victorian Town Hall was squaring its shoulders on the corner. Stephen was winding down the window.

'Don't!' I shouted. He was beyond listening, enjoying his grand gesture. 'They're my letters, I'll do what I want with them.' He chucked them out. I grabbed the wheel and yanked it towards the kerb, 'Stop the fucking car!' He slammed the brake as we slewed across the road. I'd jumped out before he could speak. The letters danced on the pavement in a light breeze, like over-sized petals. I caught one and stamped on another, as the third and fourth picked up speed away from me. Why did I need them so badly? The third wrapped itself round a railing and waited to be picked up, but the fourth was round the corner, alternately dashing and drifting, as if it was being tugged on a thread by someone who wanted to torment me. I followed it round the corner and found it headed back into the road, towards a black puddle. There was a lorry approaching. In my mind as I ran directly into the lorry's path was a plate, spinning on a stick but wobbling, tipping back and forth, its momentum almost used up. I scooped up the letter as the monster lorry thundered towards me, horn blaring. I dived one way, it swerved another, and the wind of its passing shoved me in the back. I collapsed into the gutter, panting and crying, and the kerb hit me in the jaw.

Stephen was crouching beside me.

'Why did you do that?' I gasped. 'Why?' Clutching the

letters like a bride with a ruined bouquet. 'These are all I have left. They're all I have left of him.'

In Max's room I switched on his laptop and checked my email. I had one, as I'd expected, from Clara. I skimmed it. *I'm so sorry you missed the funeral.* It was all sympathy and concern and good sense. *You're bound to feel disorientated.* I felt unconnected to her words, as if they were in a not quite familiar language. *Give Stephen a chance, he'll be reeling too.* I clicked on REPLY.

Hi Clara. So, slept with Stephen then. Why not? He's great looking and kind and a good listener and I can see exactly why Max liked him. And he's good in bed. What was great though was the human warmth, the closeness, because I've been lacking that. He's tactile, Stephen. It feels so good to be with this friend of Max's, to find some consolation together.

Actually I made it to the funeral. Loads of people there, close friends of Max, some relatives I didn't even know I had, some lovely words from the Vicar, and speeches. You should have heard all the speeches. And I've seen lots of people who say how they loved Max, no one with a bad word for him, and how he was always talking about his sister.

This version of my life was fine. If I could invent my experiences I'd be happy. If I could use telepathy to understand Stephen better and find out if Rachel was hiding anything, that might help a lot. And if I could go back in time and come home a week before Max did it, I'd be able to stop him. I stared at the screen, the blinking cursor.

Missing him. I so want to have a message from him. So want to sit down and have a quiet word with him. I want his arm round me or mine round him, want him back from the dead and happy, or not unhappy, but why shouldn't he be happy, and alive? Why shouldn't he be alive?

My fingers rested on the keyboard of Max's laptop. Just me and the screen, and the steady hum of the thing, like a yawn on a loop. Tears made me self-conscious, as if I was acting grief. I reread my email quickly—a row of brackets had appeared after *alive*, as if to apologise, to tuck the word away—then I highlighted the whole thing and clicked DELETE. Blank screen again, the winking cursor.

I wiped my face and looked out of the window where a line of seagulls started to flap their wings, all effort, no grace, rising from a roof, heading for the coast. It was still only lunch time. Lunch time and I had dreamt about Max, hadn't slept with Stephen, had told him about my mother, had read the fourth letter, had met Rachel, had participated in a shouting match, had heard about an unattractive side to my brother, had nearly been run over by a lorry, and had failed to email Clara. I closed the laptop. Silence winning out again over communication.

'We don't like each other very much and I suspect you of not being there for Max. Someone writing to you suspects you of not being there for him. We're both a little death-haunted at the moment, survivors of Max.'

'Where are you going to go?'

We sat at the kitchen table. My jaw ached where the kerb had hit it.

'Don't know,' I said. I did know. My dream about the sandcastle had given me an idea, then the last letter and something Rachel said had turned it from a whim to a definite plan. The letter had referred to *favourite places*,

Rachel had mentioned messages, and a view. The seagulls had confirmed it.

He reached across the table and touched my hair again, as he had last night. 'You're not going to do anything stupid, are you?'

It should have been dark. It should have been after midnight, both of us half-drunk and a candle flickering. It was lunch time, a long triangle of watery sun on the red formica. Toast.

'I couldn't,' Stephen continued, 'couldn't turn out the lights on everything. Could you?'

I moved my head away from his hand. 'Maybe it's in the blood,' I said. 'The family blood. You've heard the story now.'

He dropped his hand. 'But not the whole story.'

That's where we got to, Max's best friend and me. Met, didn't get on, almost had sex but didn't, split up. He was one of those men I'd sometimes wonder about in the future. What would it have been like with Stephen? Would it have been good, would it have complicated things even more? Better not to get involved. Move right along, nothing to see here. I left most of my stuff in Max's room, made Stephen promise to hang on to any further letters, and then I was in the hall. .

We faced each other and he leant a little towards me. I raised my face to his and we brushed cheeks.

'We're OK, aren't we?' he said.

I felt like asking *OK in what sense?* I didn't. I said, 'Yes, we're OK.' I felt that childish formula coming to my lips: *Thanks for having me.* I repressed it. 'Thanks for every-thing.'

Then I was gone, abruptly out of the house, as if I was being chased out. I threw my small bag into the boot.

Stephen stood in the doorway, watching. He waved as I climbed into the car.

It smelt of polish and dead smoke, like a pub just after opening. It was good to be in my own space. I placed Max's box on the passenger seat beside me and glanced at it as I drove away, wondering if it contained some portion of Max's whole story, knowing that soon I'd have to break it open. He'd left us with no choice. I laid one hand on it as I drove. The honey-coloured wood, the thread of metal wound around it, its tight curls and angles like an alphabet not yet deciphered.

Tuesday

Humans Meeting

FIRST, I HAVE TO convince the shopkeeper that I have a sincere and pressing desire. Then he lets me past the crystals, joss sticks and self-help volumes into the dark backroom. Strong scent of sandalwood in the air. A cat curled on a shelf opens one eye, watches me choose what I need. A heavy book, which I nearly drop as I pull it from the high shelf. Then a bottle, chosen from a dusty line of them, each with a Latin name handwritten in faded calligraphy. My pointing finger finds the one I want. My hand is shaking.

I have his comb with seven hairs tangled in its teeth; I have his shirt which carries, surely, flakes of his skin, residue of his sweat, a faint rumour of his smell; I have his boxers, in the cotton weave of which might lurk traces of urine, semen, shit. I have his book, *The Hobbit*, its spine wrinkled like dry skin. Page 173 is stained with his blood from the day he picked off a scab while reading. I have a fat church candle I found in his room.

Now it's midnight and I pile the artefacts beside the candle and light it. It's honey-scented and unreels a wriggling line of smoke.

So here we are then, me and Max.

The book I found in the dark backroom is as big as a phone directory, with a thick leather cover and brittle pages. The potion I found in the dark backroom is a viscous brown liquid, stinking of dead flowers. I turn to the page in the book for the ceremony, and I sing-song the words as I sprinkle the potion over his blood and hair, his skin and his fluids. *I summon you, I summon you, I beseech you, I beseech you.* My voice a low, earnest drone. Darkness, a smear of moon behind cloud, the distant whisper of the sea, and the murmur of the television from the room next door. I wait for something to happen. I want green light to swell from nowhere, smoke to billow from the candle, I want to hear my name, whispered harshly. My neighbour is listening to a quiz show; I hear a burst of applause. Nothing else. The candle flame bends in a draft, making shadows. Nothing, nothing, nothing. I fall on to my bed disappointed, feeling foolish.

Something drags me out of a deep sleep. A sound, I think, but it's gone. Silence. I begin to sink back towards unconsciousness, and then there it is again—a straining, creaking throat-noise. I open my eyes to see in the candle's flicker a long, dark shape quivering on the floor. I raise myself on one elbow. The light affords scary glimpses. The shape is wet and meaty, bound by veins and shiny ligaments. As if aware of my gaze, it starts to buckle and thrash, and now I catch sight of its face, all snarl and nose cavity and eyes that flash open and gape. That throat-noise again. Max is trying to speak, he's trying to speak to me.

Something woke me. The jaunty sound of break-fast television behind the thin wall, and the squealing of gulls. My eyes flicked open, and I lay unmoving, gasping, needing a few moments recovery time. Propped myself on an elbow and checked the floor for Max's absence. But I was pleased even then, while still recovering, pleased that Max had haunted my sleep, spun himself a story in my subconscious, pleased that he was with me now. Relaxing, untensing, I lay back and let my eyes close again.

Since leaving Hebden Bridge I'd been retelling an old

story to myself, testing it and teasing it, trying to mine every scrap of significance from it.

My last day with Max.

An amusement arcade. Harsh, synthesised coughs and growls, kids' excited yelps, the illicit feel of wasted time. The carpet mosaic of fag ends, gum and dark stains in the shape of unknown countries. We raced on Daytona, our purple cars barging into each other on steeply banked tracks; we shot zombies and weirdly mutated creatures in House of the Dead; we fed endless coins into the Flipper and the Derby and giant fruit machines with arcane rules we didn't begin to understand. The arcade was like a different country, a republic of shallow pleasures.

Max abruptly drummed his knuckles on the glass of the cabinet where I was trying to shoot dinosaurs. His face peered in at me.

'Where next, then?'

I shot at a velociraptor. 'I'm not finished.'

'Come on, we're done here.'

As always some guilt and a touch of queasiness as we left, back into the surprising daylight, the sprawl of beach in front of us.

Max said, 'It's a waste of life in there.'

'What are you talking about? You love it.'

'Waste of life.'

My last day with Max before I went to Hong Kong, and he was being difficult. We bought chips and walked in silence for a while, past the Spa to the grassy dunes beyond.

Max threw a chip up to a seagull, which swooped, caught it and flew on. 'There's something you feed seagulls,' he said, 'to make them explode. Can't remember what it is. Phosphorus?'

'Wouldn't that make them luminous?' I said.

He ignored me. 'Do you remember we saw *Live and Let Die* at the cinema here? Bond gives Mr Big a compressed air capsule, and he inflates and bursts like a balloon.'

'There was something similar in *Mary Poppins*,' I said. 'As long as they kept laughing, they kept floating. You remember? If they stopped laughing, they fell.'

'Did they just drift gently down again,' said Max, 'or did they crash?'

'Can't remember.'

'And if they were on a plane that was crashing, could they save it by laughing? And would it matter if they were laughing nervously, if it was hysteria?'

I didn't answer. He was still being difficult. He had his enigmatic face on. Max would do this—get aggressive, then go quiet and thoughtful, as if whatever was on his mind was too weighty to discuss. We climbed a sandy path, my unsuitable shoes sliding beneath me. He was walking fast, a couple of paces ahead, as if he was alone and had some particular goal in mind. I was about to shout after him, tell him to wait, tell him I needed him to be better company on our last day together.

He stopped before I could speak and let me catch up.

'I always used to dream about flying.'

'Used to?'

'Too earth-bound these days.' He flung another chip into the air where another seagull acrobatically snatched it before wheeling away. 'But let's not talk about the past. Agreed?'

'OK.'

'You know why? If we talk about the past then today will turn into the past, it'll be that time we went to the beach together, it'll become bitter-sweet. Nostalgic.'

He chewed on this last word, like it had a bad taste.

'Come on, nearly there.'

Another hundred metres up the steep path and we reached a viewpoint. The Spa, the South Bay curving as far as the old harbour, the castle on the hill above. A short stone post with a metal plaque told us how many miles it was to different cities, different countries.

'My favourite place, this,' said Max. 'I love being surrounded by all this space. And this,' he indicated the plaque, 'this is like a map suggesting places to go.'

I think I shrugged. Stephen's disease. The view was OK, and the associations of family holidays were nice, but it was cold, there was an overflowing bin a few feet away, and there were a hundred better places to be.

We sat for a while. We did speak, but I don't remember what we said. If it wasn't about the past then it was probably just films we'd seen, work prospects, life in Hong Kong. Nothing significant. Nothing about his hopes and regrets, nothing about where it was he wanted to go, nothing about whatever weighed him down and made him sad. Certainly no mention of how I felt about him. He did promise he'd visit, he promised he'd come and see me, and then we were abruptly on to the next thing. Max was always moving, as if afraid he was missing something, as if a perfect moment was just round the corner, just out of reach. We ran back down the path, back through the dunes, then past the Spa and down the slippery, treacherous steps to the beach.

Where we were faced by an unfamiliar view: a receding horizon and a big sky. 'You don't get this in England,' Max said, 'except on the coast.' And I did get a sense of what he felt then. We were looking away from our small country, towards largeness, possibility.

I picked up an old Snapple bottle as we approached the

ragged edge of the water. 'If it had a top,' I said, 'and if we had a pen and paper, we could send a message.'

He snorted. 'Childish. Better to leave a message where it might get found.'

'Like where?'

This is the crucial part of the memory, of course. Max, a year ago, still alive, giving me the clues that I need now. I asked where should you leave a message. What did he say to me? At first, I wasn't sure he'd heard. The sea was lapping at our toes, and he was gazing out towards a couple of yachts being shoved around by the wind. I don't remember his exact words. Where should you leave a message? He repeated: *Where it will be found*. Or he said: *Where it can't be missed*.

We began to build a sandcastle. He wasn't interested in sea defences, he went for height, and elaborate decoration. Then he suddenly lost interest and, fully dressed, he walked out into the water. I stayed at the sea's edge. Watched him.

'Where you heading? Norway?'

He didn't answer. He waded on, up to his knees in the North Sea. A low wave hit him. I felt a sudden unease, as if perhaps he might just keep going, I wanted to pull him back, but he shouted one loud, impassioned word, 'Bastards!' Then turned back to me.

I found the hermit crab's shell as we walked slowly across the beach. It was grimed with sand and wrapped in weed, but I washed it and shook it dry.

'I'm going to keep this,' I said, smiling at him. 'In a couple of months, I'll put it to my ear and in my little flat somewhere in the middle of Hong Kong I'll listen to you, yelling at the tide in Scarborough.'

He wasn't listening, his mind was on something else, the next thing. Sometimes when I remember that moment

I change it. I don't give him anything to say, but I have him smile back at me. It's a slow, gratified, loving smile, like an older brother ought to give to his sister.

That's all. Max and I played video games, discussed floating and flying, took on the tide, and talked about messages, favourite places. I picked up a shell as a souvenir. A week later I was on a plane, leaving the country, and the short episode was already being blurred and reshaped by memory. It was that time we went to the beach together, it was nostalgia.

I ate my full English quickly. Beans scooped up on a fatty bit of bacon, egg yolk wiped up with white toast. The landlady brought the coffee pot.

'Any plans for the day, my love?'

The only other people in the breakfast room were a couple with a baby, trying to feed it cereal. The radio was playing some sad ballad. In a different mood I'd have snapped some monosyllable at her, asked for the music to be switched off. She'd have been hurt, the couple would have looked at me disapprovingly, I'd have left feeling brittle and resentful, ready for the world to offend me.

Instead: 'We used to come here as a family,' I said. 'I'm going to revisit some old haunts.'

She looked gratified, as if this was exactly the answer she wanted to hear. I sipped coffee. Breakfast wasn't even over and it had already been a good day. Perhaps, after all, this would end up as a story that could be pieced together with clues. You go from person to person asking questions. *What happened? What can you tell me?* You interrogate your own recollections, you interpret hints and implications like a detective.

The fourth letter mentioned favourite places, then Rachel said Max told her about a family trip to

Scarborough, said he mentioned messages in bottles. Max deliberately showed me his favourite place and told me messages should be left where they would be found. My first dream had me and Max on the beach in Scarborough, my second dream had Max returning to me, trying to speak to me.

Hints and implications. It was a place to begin, perhaps a way to breathe life back into my brother.

I left the B&B, seen off with a cheerful wave from the landlady, and began to retrace the journey Max and I had taken a year ago. The arcade. I loitered briefly among the lights and the loud machines. A pale boy said something to me and laughed, something I didn't catch, but I swore at him to make him keep his distance. I was on the promenade, I'd barely begun, when the first strange thing happened. A horn blared at me as I hurried across the road, I shouted something at the driver, turned back to the kerb and nearly walked into the arms of Greg Davidson.

'I recognise you,' he said. 'Saw you in a rush, looking mad at someone, thought, I know that girl.'

I stared at him, too surprised to speak. Took a step back.

'We met on the plane, you recall?'

I was still staring, but managed a nod. The fat American with the mustard stain. Today he looked smarter, unstained and less crumpled.

'Now, you're not going to give me the silent treatment again, are you? The name's Greg; maybe you found my card?'

A smile in his eyes, as if he knew more than I did.

'Yes,' I said, 'I found your card. My name's Gloria.'

'Gloria.' He seemed to swill the name in his mouth like wine. 'How about a coffee, Gloria? My treat.'

'I'm busy, on my way somewhere.'

'Mind if I come along? I'm at a conference here, I've got the afternoon off. Be nice to spend some time with a friendly face.'

'I wasn't friendly last time we met.'

'Maybe you will be this time.'

He had that wide smile some Americans have—open and warm and expecting only good things. Why not? Why shouldn't he come with me? We walked together to the Spa. Strange, lifeless buildings. A poster advertising a singer, line-dancing. I told Greg that I'd been weeping on the plane for my brother. I told him that I thought he'd left a message for me, and now I knew where to find it. We climbed the steep, sandy path towards the viewpoint. Greg was taking it slowly, some steps behind me. I was gasping, eager but unfit, my heavy bag containing Max's laptop and his box banging on my hip, as I approached the stone mushroom. Where would you leave a message? *Where it will be found.*

'Surely that means his favourite place?' I said to Greg. 'Don't you think?'

He nodded, unsure.

'This is good in fact, this is good, because there were two of us on that day, me trailing along behind, like you. No offence.'

Greg smiled at my excitement, but I could see he was concerned, I could see he was anticipating disappointment. I didn't want his sympathy, so I concentrated on my task.

The stubby post of dark stone pierced the earth, as if a giant had been buried below us with his raised thumb exposed to the sky. On its angled top the metal plate still gave the number of miles to London, New York and Sydney. I crouched in front of it, like an acolyte before a shrine, put both hands on it and moved my palms over its cool grain. Slowly, I shuffled round it, still squatting, ignoring the ache in my calves and thighs, until I found what I hoped for. A crevice where the mortar had crumbled, a dark slit between the stones. Was there something in there? I searched the ground for a twig, wriggled it in and tried to use it as a hook. There was something there, but I was pushing it back.

'This is it,' I said to Greg over my shoulder, triumphant. 'Max has left me a note.'

I tried to angle the twig, tried to insert my fingernail, touched the edge of something, paper, scraped at it, nudged it away then tugged it back, then finally teased out a tiny corner, pincered it between my nails and slid it from its hiding place.

I held the folded sheet of paper a moment, breathing hard, close to tears. Max's letter to me; his last words. I unfolded the paper. Stared at what I saw as if through staring I could conjure something more. I saw nothing. No words. It was a sketch of a bird, pointy beaked, hungry, with a fierce glare. I couldn't even be certain (but I *was* certain) that it was his.

'Max.' I heard myself whisper his name. Greg crouched beside me. I rested my head on his chest and he laid his arm round my shoulders.

We walked slowly back down the path. He said he was sorry, that consoling hand of his resting on my wrist.

'What exactly do you want from your brother?'

We were on the beach, walking on wet, hard-packed sand. I was trying to find a clear answer to this question, when the second strange thing happened. Walking towards us was a red-head in an anorak.

'I don't believe this,' said Robbie. 'Gloria, right? How's it going?'

I looked from Greg to Robbie. Again, I couldn't speak.

'Robbie. Remember me?'

Something was going on. 'Where have you come from? I don't understand.'

'I've got a car. My mate gave it me, cos he felt bad about the whole band thing.'

I shook my head, as if to shake the irrelevance out. 'So?'

'So I'm on the M62, and the sun's shining, and I think, I'll go to the beach.'

I was just staring at him, not sure whether to feel pleased or paranoid. 'Something's going on. What's going on?'

'Perhaps I'll leave,' said Greg. 'I'm sorry the message didn't work out.'

I tried to refocus my attention on to him. 'You said you had the afternoon off?'

'I should get back. But I hope you'll be in touch?'

I said I would, he wished me good luck, and then he walked away, across the sand. I had no time to recover from Greg, because Robbie was in my face.

'So, you all right then?'

This was strange. If it was coincidence, then it was coincidence with a shape and a structure. But I couldn't work out how these meetings could have been engineered.

'What do you mean, am I all right?'

'Everything OK?'

'Sure.'

He didn't seem particularly pleased to hear this, as if he'd expected something else. He didn't seem particularly surprised to see me either.

'Right,' he said, 'what's been happening?'

We sat on the sand, him in his anorak and jeans, me in shorts and a vest. The sun eased me on to my back and I spoke without looking at him as he lay beside me.

The sky was bright and dazzling, so I closed my eyes. I found myself telling him everything, found it all spilling out, about the letters, about Max sleeping with Jude and wanting to sleep with Rachel, about him being a bad friend as well as a bad brother, about sleeping beside Stephen but not getting on with him, and about failing to find any message from Max.

'And you're feeling what? Pissed off?'

He should have been solemn, impressed by my story, but he wasn't. I didn't answer.

'See, this is what I said, remember? I said my brother was a wanker, and yours sounds like one too.'

I had no answer to that either. My fingers wormed into the sand, grains gritted under my nails.

Robbie seemed impatient. 'But you're not about to do anything, are you? Anything stupid?'

I looked at him. 'What?'

'Like top yourself?'

I was struck again by the unlikeliness of his presence, his concern. 'What are you doing here, Robbie?'

'I owed you one,' he said.

Now I was impatient with him, with his unwillingness to answer my questions. I took off my shoes, started to take off my shorts. I remembered my brief fear that he was going to rape me. That seemed ridiculous now, sitting next to this earnest boy wearing his anorak in the sunshine.

He sat up as I stripped. 'What you doing?'

'Going for a swim.'

'You can't do that.'

'You coming?'

To my surprise, he was. As I stood, he took off his anorak, pulled off his trainers, started hopping out of his jeans, muttering that this was mad and stupid, that he wished he'd never seen me and he was a crap swimmer. Sunbathers watched us, amused: me down to bra and knickers, him in his boxers, heading for the sea. We got to the edge and I kept going, as Max had a year ago, Robbie trailing after me reluctantly. 'We seriously don't want to be doing this.' I ignored him, wading on, cold and shivery but determined, gasping as the water reached my crotch, and then diving in, hearing Robbie say, 'Oh fuck!' as he followed.

The water was a cold hand, squeezing me, salt stung my eyes and slid up my nose. I shook my head, ducked under and kicked out towards the horizon, then suddenly felt fingers round my ankle, pulling me back. I stood and turned, ready to be angry, but Robbie was laughing, his mood finally improving, so I pushed him instead and shoved his head beneath the surface, then tried to swim away as he chased me, shouting.

It wasn't what I'd imagined. In landlocked Hebden Bridge I'd had thoughts of a long, solitary swim, of treading the deep, cold water a few hundred yards from the shore and resting there, between land and sea, life and death, coming to a decision. I'd imagined seeing the sunbathers, small and insignificant and far away, imagined feeling that everything was far away. It would have been dignified. I shrieked as Robbie splashed me, jumped on his back as he turned away and pulled him over into the water. His boxers came off and he backed away, scrabbling them up again as I laughed and leapt away from him like a seal.

When I stepped out of the water, shedding it like a dress, I was shivering again, all but naked. Getting dry was a question of shaking ourselves and standing, limbs outstretched, in the unreliable sun.

'That was great,' said Robbie. 'That was better than I

thought.' Now he was like a kid on holiday, excited and gauche. 'And I don't know if you even noticed, but I just have to say,' he nodded down towards his boxers, 'it's not usually that small. That was just the cold water.'

I laughed again. I was used to men taking themselves more seriously than this: Max, Stephen. Robbie made a refreshing change.

As the tide came in, we built an elaborate sandcastle. It had a high turret with shells for windows, and pebbles inset along the wall facing the approaching sea. On the turret, a boiled sweet wrapper on a lolly stick rustled in the breeze.

The sea arrived, gentle at first, nudging and licking the dry sand, then more insistent, splashing against the sides, creating small breaches, splashing over the top. We dug desperately and shored up the undermined walls, sacrificed the high turret to repair a hole, becoming more involved as the sea ringed the walls entirely, cutting us off from dry land.

Something miraculous happened. The walls held, we stayed dry, the sea jostled pointlessly around us for a while, and then began its long retreat. The castle accidentally avoided becoming a glorious failure. We looked at each other, surprised and a little embarrassed.

Robbie checked his watch. 'So you're all right, yeah?'

'I'm fine.'

'Cos there's somewhere I should be.'

'Robbie, why are you here? Really?'

He jumped out of the sandcastle, headed up the beach. 'You did me a big favour. Now we're even.'

We parted on a side street off the promenade. He made me promise to ring him, then drove off in his wreck of a car, belching smoke.

After that, when the third strange thing happened, I

wasn't as shocked as I might have been. James was sitting in his wheelchair outside a pub, drinking lager from a straw. I walked up to his table, sat down with him and said hello. I might have been less casual if I'd known that the biggest shock of the day was still to come.

His smile shivered around his lips, as if out of focus.

'James, what's going on? It's good to see you, but what's going on? I keep meeting people I know.'

'Your friend called. Stephen. Worried about you. Said you were here.'

So much for coincidence. 'Worried? What sort of worried?'

'He found something you wrote. Thought you were going to,' he indicated the sea. 'Drown.'

Waking in Max's bed one night, I'd transcribed a half–remembered dream. The long, solitary swim.

'Well, where is he then?'

'Don't know. Looking for you?'

It was unsettling. Stephen was stalking me by proxy. He must have called Greg and Robbie, must have been in my room looking through my things. Perhaps he liked to pilfer too. James said he was supposed to pretend it was coincidence if we met, he was supposed to just gauge my mood and look after me if necessary.

'So, not about to kill yourself?' he asked.

'No. This is embarrassing. Change the subject.'

We talked about Scarborough and video games, sand–castles, Greg and Robbie, the weather, swimming and his sister, who was apparently wandering up and down side streets, looking for me. Inconsequential, easy talk that felt like lying down and taking a long, deep breath.

I told James why I was here and showed him the drawing of the bird: a few swift lines, that wide eye.

'What did you want?' he said. 'From Max?'

Greg's question. 'I wanted him to write me a message saying he loved me, and I was a good sister, and he's sorry.'

James's shrug involved the whole upper half of his body.

'If he could say all that . . .'

I completed the thought. 'Maybe he wouldn't have done it, I know. We don't communicate in my family.'

He lifted his hand towards me, pointing. 'You do.'

'No.'

'Remember, I watch. I watch humans meeting.'

I found myself irritated. 'Believe me, in my family we don't do communication.'

I told him about my mother. When I wanted to, I could make those odd habits and eccentric episodes sound comic. Most stories, if they're edited right, can come out sounding harmless and funny, anecdote-material. I avoided this, gave James the story straight, as a sequence of events with a natural shape to it, with a darkening mood and a clear conclusion. I told him what happened after our father died, how our mother was diagnosed, what happened after that.

'When Stella died, in a hospital, she thought the CIA were after her. She was dying but she wouldn't speak to us, because of the listening device they'd implanted inside her. She wouldn't speak to us. That's what Max and I inherited.'

I felt self-conscious. It was a story I didn't tell often, and now I'd told it twice in two days.

'You met me,' said James, with effort. 'Greg, Robbie. Communicated. Must have. We came to help.'

'Greg had a conference. Robbie didn't really want to be here.'

Leaning towards me, his elbows on the table, his eyes

still in his unstill face. He insisted, 'It's about humans, meeting.'

Philosophies. Clara thinks life is about giving and receiving love, Stephen seems to think it's about finding the right relationship, James thinks it's about humans meeting, I've always thought it's about spinning plates. Max was the plate that crashed and upset everything. I didn't want to explain to James though, how difficult it is to accommodate change in your life. I guessed he knew.

Behind him, his sister approached.

'You found her,' she said.

I was embarrassed again, had to explain that no I wasn't suicidal, that I was grateful they'd come, and yes, I'd be fine now, I'd be fine. Like Greg and Robbie they had other things they should be doing, had taken time out in response to Stephen's call. They went. James with that wobbly smile, his sister puzzled; they left me at the pub, with my unfinished beer.

Were Katie, Jude and Rachel going to show up next? I wasn't sure whether to be angry with Stephen or touched. Ever since I'd arrived in England, I'd been doing my usual thing, trying to skirt the messy and the personal, not give myself away; now I'd been ambushed by other people's concern. I sipped my drink as I watched James leave. In front of me, Max's laptop and his metal-wrapped wooden box with its tantalising contents. My new plan was to throw the box under the wheels of the next car, let it be destroyed so that I could find the note that might be inside.

That was the moment. I was looking at Max's laptop and the box. I was thinking about communication in my family, and the lack of it. The last words I hadn't received from Max. That was the moment. I froze, my glass on its way to my mouth. A thought had hit me, a thought about the letters which made me want to phone Stephen immediately.

My seat clattered back. I threw down some change and was gone. My mobile was back in my room, I couldn't see a phone box, so I half walked, half ran up the side street alongside the café on to a busy road. I waited to cross, watched a coach approaching, tapping my foot, almost dancing with impatience. The coach was pale green and cream, it said *Malton* on the front and the driver wore sunglasses.

That's when the strangest thing on that strange day happened.

A hole opened in the road and the coach rushed in. It wasn't quite that it fell in, it was more as if it lurched into it down a steep ramp, scraping its undercarriage on the lip. Screech of metal, spray of sparks, snatches of faces in window after window, like a jerky piece of film, the hole widening, half-swallowing the whole bus like a snake with a raccoon. And wasn't that Stephen? One of those shocked faces. Was that Stephen?

Story of a Hero

STEPHEN SWITCHED ON his light and sat up, squinting and trembling. Two in the morning. Sleep was difficult lately, and if he managed it he always seemed to have bad dreams. He looked at his computer.

Yawning, pulling on a thin sweater, sliding his hands up and down his face, he waited for the screen to come to life. Then he wrote five words: *Stories I Haven't Told Gloria*. He underlined the title, put it into bold, then back into plain text, then into italics. He hit Return twice. Then he wondered where to start. Stories I haven't told Gloria? It was his whole life, potentially. Under his first title he wrote: *Stories I Haven't Told Gloria About Max*. Put it in bold, hit Return. Still no good. There were too many. From, How I Met Max on to Max's Funeral. And all those moments—Pub Lunch With Max, Watching TV With Max, Argument With Max—all those casual, unnoticed moments in between. Stephen moved the mouse back and forth, frustrated, making the cursor reel around like a fly trapped behind the screen. There could be no whole story of course, not for Max, not for anyone. There were only stories, a few odd pieces of an elaborate jigsaw, hinting at the rest of the pattern. A patch of grey which might be stone or sky; a complicated blue, either river or that door, painted with shadow.

Under his first two titles Stephen wrote a third: *My Last Evening With Max*.

They'd argued. Stephen had gone into Max's room and found him lying on the floor. Stephen was busy, he was marking and he'd only come to borrow a pen, but when he saw Max he abruptly said, 'Tell me something you like about yourself.' He didn't know where this had come from, but he was pleased with it, it sounded like something a therapist might say.

Max just stared at the ceiling for a few seconds, his fingernails in the carpet, and Stephen thought he was going to ignore the question, but he finally spoke. 'I like my name,' he said. And he explained how if you forced it a little it started as a kiss then turned into a smile. 'It's a good trick for a name,' he said.

'What else?' Stephen felt this was going well. 'What else do you like?'

'My body, of course,' Max said. This was a joke between them. 'It's the body I would have chosen if I'd been shown an album and asked to pick one.' Max was tall and lean and fit, with dark, almost black hair.

He stared at the ceiling, considering, flicking his cheek with his fingernails.

'And what else?'

The pause stretched. His ideas had run dry. He raised one arm. It looked languid but it wasn't, he was concentrating. He had this thing where he'd lie on his back and raise an arm straight up and try to balance it there. It stayed there a moment, fingers hanging in gravity, then fell on to the thin carpet. He didn't look lean and fit, he looked like someone who was trying to treat a chronic back problem, a deep, stubborn ache.

Stephen set aside his marking and dragged Max down to the pub. They walked down the hill into Hebden, Stephen talking about summer and his script and plans for the future. He pointed out the blue hydrangea Max sometimes admired, overflowing a garden, noticed a cat stretched along a wall on Lee Mill Road, that looked like the snapped cat Max had been carrying when they first met.

In The White Lion, Stephen brought a couple of pints to their table and sat down, wondering what to say next. Sipped his drink. After a few moments Max shook his head, said: 'You and Jude.'

'What?'

And Max started on about how what Stephen needed was a girlfriend, because basically he'd never got over Jude, and he'd taken it out on Rachel, and what he really needed was to sort out his attitude to women and then move on, move on, because his life seemed to have stalled after Jude.

Stephen had resented the lecture. 'Don't have a go at me because you're feeling bad.'

'I'm not feeling bad.'

Stephen just looked at him.

'All right, I am feeling bad, but that gives me clarity of vision.'

'You think?'

'I know, I know, I know.' He tapped his temple. 'Clarity.'

'If you had clarity, Max, or anything like clarity, you'd sort yourself out.'

'How?'

'I don't know. Get some therapy, get a job.'

'Right, that should fix everything.'

They'd drunk their pints. Stephen bought another round. It wasn't much of a story. Stephen wasn't sure what else they'd talked about. They were brooding now, and didn't have much to say to each other. In recent days he'd reviewed every second of their encounter, wishing that instead of talking about himself and hydrangeas and cats, he'd found the moment and the will to say the warm, uplifting or encouraging thing which might have made the difference. *Get some therapy, get a job.* That certainly wasn't warm, uplifting or encouraging. It had been a crucial moment, and he'd failed to recognise it. They'd drunk two pints each and gone home. In the hall, as he locked the door, Stephen had said three words from which he now took meagre comfort.

'Have a coffee?'

Max paused on the stairs. 'I'm going to read.'

'You haven't got any books.'

'Then I'm going to think.'

Max went up to his room. Stephen watched him go up to his room.

He shouted to him to wait, he ran after him and went into his room, he got Katie to come over, he called Gloria, he put an arm round Max's shoulders and sat and talked long into the night with him, stumbling through a forest of words, discovering an eloquence and sensitivity and insight he never knew he possessed, finally reaching some sort of tentative resolution. There was a hug, there were tears, there was a sense that their friendship had been redefined, that it was a solid and substantial thing that could be relied on, that could not be considered flawed.

Max went up to his room. Stephen stood, silent and irritated, thinking about his marking, watching him go up to his room.

His life was absences now. The empty house spoke to him, its shifts and grumbles keeping him awake. Max was a heat haze at midnight, a ripple in the air, a rustle by the window. Back in bed, but sleepless, Stephen tried to think of Gloria, another absence, imagining what could have been, and should have been, with her. *We don't like each other very much.* Perhaps not, but they might have thrived without words, communicating through movement and weight and shifts of pressure. The pressure changed inside Stephen, and he found his image of Gloria disturbed by a memory of Rachel, on the rug, framed by sunlight. That moment had been light, happy, connected; everything that this moment wasn't. Rachel was a third absence, another prompt for guilt and regret. She'd loved him. When had that happened, and why hadn't he noticed? He was thirty-three, he'd chatted and joked with her and made love, he'd become irritated by her and casually dropped her. How could it be that he was thirty-three years old and knew nothing?

Insomnia was the last thing he needed. Guilt and self-loathing were the last things he needed too. He was seeing Tim Griffin in the morning, he wanted to be alert, artic-ulate, interesting — all the things he'd failed to be with Gloria, with Rachel, and perhaps with Max. He thought about things he could do to pass the time — read, get on the Internet, watch television, make a cathedral out of matchsticks. He moved his mind from Rachel, naked in sunlight, to the slow, meticulous work of building some-thing substantial out of matches. Not a project he'd ever tried, but he could imagine himself doing it. You'd have an impossibly fine paintbrush for your glue, you'd strike and extinguish match after match, you'd work to a design, watching your project develop, the burnt, caramel smell lingering around you. He saw his cathedral in a pool of light in a dark room, the product of countless hours of effort: a fortified, breakable edifice.

'Open, friendly, relaxed.' He breathed the words aloud to himself, as he left Victoria station, heading past the massive

Marks and Spencers, into Manchester. He was trying to trick himself into feeling self-assured, even urbane. Difficult when he was so tired. What had Gloria said to him? Acting confident was very like being confident. Nice idea. He wondered if Griffin had guessed how closely the script mirrored his own life.

Rose and Simon are finishing a meal in a restaurant. There's a tense silence before Rose speaks.

ROSE: You'd call yourself, what? Happy?

SIMON: I'd call myself tired. Can't we go home, do this in the morning?

ROSE: Happy or not?

SIMON: Not. Not exactly.

ROSE: Why not, why aren't you happy with me?

SIMON: That's not what I said. Why is it when I talk to women I feel like I'm getting verbal slaps in the face all the time?

ROSE: Yes, why is that, I wonder?

SIMON: You and me . . .

He can't complete the sentence.

ROSE: Yes?

Beat. He shrugs.

SIMON: Sorry.

ROSE: You're dumping me. Is that right, are you dumping me?

SIMON: Got it in one.

ROSE: You're a shit.

SIMON: I'm not, I'm complicated.

ROSE: Why are you being like this?

SIMON: I don't know. Maybe I saw your stuff all over the house, and panicked. Or maybe I'm just bored.

Rose picks up her wine glass and throws the wine in his face.

The gesture doesn't seem to give her much pleasure. She leaves, Simon slowly dries his face.

It felt good to walk in the city. Sometimes Hebden Bridge, nesting in its high-sided valley, inhabited by familiar faces, could become oppressive. It felt good to find noise and traffic and sour-faced strangers around him. He paused outside shop windows, browsed briefly in Waterstones, took his time.

Then he was outside the building, and hesitating, wondering if his life was going to change while he was in there, over the next hour or so, if he was going to come out a different person, with a different future. He paused, took a deep breath, then entered the double doors.

'What I like here is not really your story, it's the characters. Actually it's not the characters either, not your main ones, it's the little people, at the edges. You know what I mean? When you step back from telling your story, shovelling it along like snow off a path, suddenly these smaller characters have got room to move. I like your waitresses, their little tête-à-tête, very nice.'

Open, friendly, relaxed. Stephen thanked him, started to say something about how he began with character. Griffin smiled and interrupted, asked him what he liked watching on television. Griffin was a short man in white T-shirt and black jeans. He had a boyish face and hair cut short like a footballer. He moved his hand now and then over his scalp, as if the cut was new and he was pleased with it. He met Stephen's eye and seemed to listen, but there was a problem. Stephen didn't feel he was communicating, he was aware of occupying a small niche of Griffin's day, of being one of many people Griffin would see that week.

He picked up his coffee from the awkwardly low table, sipped it, then lied about watching a series he'd read about. It involved a group of people in their thirties, their relationships, the incidents in their lives. He said it was funny and clever and involving and then, watching Griffin's face, he added that he felt it could be more risk-taking, that it wasn't memorable, and really he'd like to write something memorable.

Griffin looked him in the eye again, smiled again, and suddenly Stephen wondered if he was being laughed at. 'Memorable, yes. We'd all like that, wouldn't we?' Stephen felt his words were washing against Griffin like waves against a cliff. There was something about his easy manner; he was like a doctor holding back his diagnosis, letting the patient ramble on for a while about his symptoms.

'My friend died,' he said.

Griffin raised his eyebrows.

'Sorry if I'm not being, you know, articulate, but my friend just died, the funeral was only a couple of days ago. He killed himself.'

'I'm sorry.'

'I think what happens is, you keep functioning and you underestimate the effect, because you seem to be just carrying on.'

Griffin's easy manner was pleasingly disturbed. 'We don't have to continue with this.'

'But I would like to do something memorable. Write something, I mean.'

They spoke some more. Stephen stumbled out a few experiences of memorable television, all of which seemed to come from his childhood, then Griffin looked at his watch, nodded at Stephen's last reminiscence, and said, 'Anyway.'

They both got up, shook hands. Griffin waved Stephen's script at him.

'I like this, but not enough. Send me another. We might get you a trial script on something, we might find you a story-lining job. Or we might not. What do you do, teach? I admire teachers enormously, I couldn't do it.' And Stephen was back on the street, outside the building again, with a disgruntled sense of having achieved nothing at all. He checked his watch. He'd been in there slightly less than half an hour. He felt as if he had a secret he was keen to pass on, one that would clarify and impress and even delight, but somehow the right question had never quite been asked, or the right answer had never quite been formulated. The secret remained secret, something for him to mull over and brood on, when what he longed to do was tell the world.

He'd planned to see a film, eat tapas, buy some shoes, generally make the most of a day in the city. He didn't. He walked straight back to the station, as if he was in a hurry, and caught the next train home.

Hall, kitchen, sitting room, bedroom. He moved from one to the next, put the kettle on, turned the TV on then off again, found himself sitting on the edge of his bed. The mattress was too soft, he needed a new one. The blanket should be folded away in a cupboard, not rucked up at the end of the bed. He wasn't, in any sense, where he wanted to be, that was the problem. He thought about calling Rachel, but his mood was wrong, he'd probably only make her angry again. Lack of communication, that was the problem. Katie would talk to him if she wasn't busy, but it would feel feeble to call her. Where did he want to be? Perhaps in Max's room, now Gloria's room. She'd looked through his stuff, found the teeth and the hair, now he'd look for her secrets.

ENGLISH FRIENDS?
Greg Davidson.
Robbie.
James.
Katie.
Jude.
Rachel.

The list was lying on Max's desk, written in pencil on a lined pad. She'd drawn an outline of her hermit crab's shell at the bottom of the page. Who were Greg Davidson and Robbie? When had she met them? Next to the pad, under the shell, lay Greg Davidson's business card, and scraps of paper bearing phone numbers. She was making herself a circle of friends, starting to envisage an English life. What was Jude doing on the list? Had Gloria been lying about not liking her? And why wasn't he on the list? He pulled open her wardrobe, rifled through her clothes. She hadn't cleared herself a space at one end of the rail, she'd hung her shirts and her dress between Max's shirts, laying claim to the whole wardrobe. Typical. He kicked open her suitcase, looked under her pillow, opened the drawer of the bedside table. More leafs from Max's pad. She'd written something on one of them. Her handwriting was that loopy girl's writing, but small and sloping as if scribbled quickly, while the impulse was fresh.

I'm swimming out, strong strokes towards the horizon, exhausting myself. The sea is lifting against me in smooth, muscular swells, and it's an effort to make progress, but when I look back I see I've moved far away from the shore. Not far enough. I want to be further out, I don't want the temptation of returning, I want to be out at the far edge of myself, I want to be lost.

Stephen stared at this, wondered if it was a dream or a fantasy. *Death-haunted*, she'd said. He was afraid for her suddenly, lurching out of the house alone. *Maybe it's in the blood*, she'd said. *You've heard the story*. Stella's story, Max's story. *Thanks for everything*. Was there a deliberate finality in those words? He'd done nothing but fight with her since she'd arrived, and now she'd gone and if something happened to her it would be his fault, he'd have let her down as he'd perhaps let her brother down. He picked up the phone by the bed and rang her mobile. No answer. He tried to think logically. He could call the police. But first he should call Greg, and those other phone numbers. But before that he should think about what she'd said.

He thought instead of when he'd first caught sight of her, shouting at a passing pedestrian outside the house. Stirred up, face clenched, fists waving. That was a good way to see her — close enough to get a sense of her, but out of range. She was all gusts and intermittent calms. Where might this latest gust have taken her? *I'm swimming out*. She'd mentioned a place where she'd been happy, then Rachel had mentioned it too. He picked up the shell — it had probably come from the beach at Scarborough.

He phoned Greg, Robbie, James. He must have gabbled, he must have conveyed the urgency. They were surprised and confused. Greg was fortuitously on the spot; Robbie was reluctant but seemed to think Stephen was calling in a favour; James was concerned. All seemed to understand that something important was happening, and they were needed. (*And by the way*, he wanted to say, *who are you? Who are you and why do you care?*) It felt good to have a mission. He checked train times, calculated it would be quicker than driving, stuffed some things in a bag and was out of the house. The train was leaving in minutes, he'd have to move fast. It felt good to be in motion. (But would she be there?) It felt good to be acting on an impulse, with a definite aim in mind. (And how would he find her if she was there?) He parked illegally in the station car park, jumped out and sprinted for the platform, hero in his own story. The train was in, the guard was getting back on. Stephen yelled and the guard turned and looked at him wearily, unimpressed by his urgency, his starring role in the drama of train-catching. He waited though, he waited as Stephen ran up, panted a thank you, and stepped on board. He was on his way, on his way to save Gloria's life.

The train pulled out and for a while he was impatient, still tense, fidgeting, wanting to stride up and down the aisle. Slowly though, he began to relax, he'd done everything he could, slowly his tiredness crept up on him, there was nothing more he could do. He slept. Having been awake half the night he slept through the frequent stops and the uneven noise as the scenery changed and the sun alternately dazzled and disappeared. He slept for over an hour until the train juddered to a halt and he woke with a start, disorientated, wondering where he was.

He looked out of the window, bleary and slow. He was nowhere. Between stations, in nondescript landscape, stationary. He sat up, anxiety returning. There was a woman diagonally opposite him.

'Where are we? What's happened?'

She just looked at him, murmured something, possibly 'Don't know'. There was an announcement, barely intelligible, from the guard. Something was defective, he heard the word *train*, he heard the word *points*. So much for his drama, where he was bold and purposeful, Gloria's saviour. He'd had an image of catching her as she waded out, reasoning with her as waves crashed around them, bringing her back, grateful and abashed, to dry land. He hadn't had an image of sitting on a train, looking through a grimy window, relying on three putative friends, two of whom he'd never met or heard of, one of whom was a wheelchair-user, and would hardly be able to physically restrain Gloria.

His muscles were tensing at the thought, he was gripping the edge of the table as he imagined pulling her back from the greedy, sucking sea. He sighed angrily and took out the letters, hoping to distract himself while he waited for the train to move again. He'd snatched them up as he left, knowing their importance to Gloria ('They're all I have left of him'), thinking they might be useful.

One. *Your best friend's dead, you could start by telling the truth, you're a disaster with women.* Two. *He killed himself. I know why, you know too.* Three. *Is she like Max, (except a better person in every way)? Are you likely to sleep with her?* Four. *You didn't know Max, the experiences that define him, Want to know more? Ask Rachel.*

The anonymous writer's greatest hits. The four dirty, wrinkled letters, stained with bath water and breakfast and street grime, one of them half-shredded by a bread knife, lay in front of Stephen. He tried to imagine what would have happened if they'd never arrived. He'd be quietly trying to accommodate Max's death; Gloria might have returned to Hong Kong by now; he certainly wouldn't recently have seen Jude and Rachel; wouldn't have called Greg, Robbie and James; wouldn't be on this train, waiting to get to Scarborough. His life surely wouldn't have this unsettled, challenging, frankly unnerving quality.

He tried to concentrate. The writer knew him and knew Max, and seemed to know Rachel. What about Katie, could it be her? On the principle that the culprit was always the least likely person, it should be her, but he couldn't imagine her being so callous or so manipulative. She'd just come out and say what she wanted to say. And anyway, the writer hinted that they knew Gloria.

He was getting an idea. Why wouldn't the writer just meet him face to face and tell him these things? He was getting an idea, and it seemed both absurd and obvious simultaneously. He took out his mobile, having trouble in his excitement with Gloria's number. Still no answer. Where was she? He looked out of the window and found that they were moving, he'd been too engrossed to notice, they were moving and soon, if only Greg or Robbie or James had found her, he'd be able to tell Gloria something astonishing.

His mistake was to ask for directions. He'd decided to head for the beach—he'd told the others that that was where they should look for Gloria in case she was swimming out to sea, so he was going to follow his own advice. If he'd looked he'd have found signs clearly pointing the way, but instead he asked a teenager who was either ignorant or mischievous, because she sent him off in another direction, over a bridge and up a tree-lined hill, and after he'd walked for a while he realised he must have gone wrong. When he stopped someone else, they asked him if he wanted the North or South Bay and he started to panic, realising how unlikely it was that he would find one woman in a large town. She suggested he get a bus into the centre, pointed him towards a stop. That's how he came to be on the green and cream coach.

The driver, inscrutable behind sunglasses, took his money, and Stephen took a window seat towards the back. He was trying to work out a plan, trying to revive that sense of himself as the star of the drama of saving Gloria, but he'd only got as far as heading out to the water's edge and staring out to sea, when it happened. The dull, steady progress of the bus was interrupted by a jolt—he thought they'd hit something—and then there was a downward lurch and his head struck the rail on the seat in front. There was time to think he was going to die. And it felt ironic because he'd intended to save Gloria, but he wasn't a star now, just an expendable extra. And he thought it was like an aeroplane, not a bus, because of the sudden spill downwards. And there was a ferocious scraping sound, like metal being cut on a lathe by a blunt saw. And it all lasted only a fraction of a second. Now he was gripping the rail he'd hit with his head so when the bus stopped, when it abruptly slammed into something which halted it, he was catapulted off his seat, but he kept hanging on to the rail, he hung on and was lifted into the air but not thrown forwards, not hurled towards the driver, who was currently hanging out of his shattered windscreen, hanging into a fissure in the earth, instead he did a muscle-wrenching loop, like a monkey on a bar, landing up on the seat in front, breathless and confused but alive, still alive, alive enough to wonder what in the world had just happened.

Wednesday

Margin

ONE DAY, HE'D tell this story. A man waits outside a chapel to bury his friend. Thinking old, tired thoughts about death. Inside, slow music is playing, and other people's faces are closed and far away.

Stephen was awake. He was not awake. Stephen was dreaming again. But he could smell the starch of the pillow case, feel the stiff, clean material against his cheek. He must be awake, so he wasn't dreaming, he was remembering the story that one day he would tell.

He was dawdling outside the chapel with the others, not sure whether to enter. They couldn't wait any longer, for Gloria. Stephen had organised the funeral, but there was an aunt there and she had precedence. So someone approached the aunt. Would she like to go in before the coffin, or after?

They lined up in the pews, the coffin laid perpendicular to them, in front of curtains. Low voices, phatic exchanges, empty of meaning. There was a scraping. *Scritch, scritch, scritch.* Quiet, but distinct. You could tell who had heard and who hadn't: a slow wave of silence worked backwards, filling the chapel. People looked around, there was an anxious laugh. Still the scraping. *Scritch, scritch, scritch.* Heads turned slowly, reluctantly, towards the coffin. Finally, as if someone had signalled, there was consternation. Stephen stood up, several people stood up, then they were prising off the lid. They lifted it off and dropped it, it clattered on the floor, and they stepped back. A pause. Everyone staring, every breath in the chapel held.

With a yowl, a dark cat sprang out of the coffin. It had no tail.

Stephen was not awake, he was dreaming. But when he opened his eyes he could see a jug of water on a bedside table. He must be awake, he must be remembering. They put the lid back on, and the cat curled up on top of it. It eyed the seated mourners, bared its claws and hissed at any hand raised against it. Stephen wondered—was the cat Max, or was it Gloria? He let his head fall back to gaze at the ceiling of the chapel. He saw a spider. OK, the spider must be Max. But Stephen was afraid of spiders. Gloria then, the spider must be Gloria.

He had phoned friends and the aunt, he'd chosen the music. He'd had the chapel stripped of its crosses because Max, as far as he knew, was an atheist. Something else they'd never discussed. A nice woman with a patronising voice read a poem. There was a ship involved and a harbour, but Stephen didn't understand a word of it. Someone sang. Someone sang and that's what started him crying, suddenly he was shuddering and tears were rolling down his face, which was bad luck because it was his turn to speak.

Was he awake now, or dreaming? He was in some marginal place between. Maybe he was inventing this story, and maybe it was true anyway.

'For what we are about to receive . . .' No, he didn't say that. He stood at the front, people gazing at him. He'd learnt a speech, he had a piece of paper with notes to prompt him. He was going to talk about his friendship with Max, how much it meant to him, how lucky he felt that Max had been in his life. He was going to identify

Max's key qualities—humour and audacity—and tell a story to illustrate them. He looked at the paper he was holding. His notes had disappeared. The paper said: *So now what are you going to do?*

He was awake. A nurse leaning over him. Pale blue. For some reason he was telling her, in a whisper, about Gloria.

'I mean her name. It's like some sort of Roman war cry, isn't it? Either that, or it's a little old lady's name. She can't get to her brother's funeral, chooses a plane that cuts it too fine. It's been a week, nearly, and we've hardly said a kind word. But I've got something to tell her now, because I know something, I know something . . .'

'Stephen,' the nurse said, 'go to sleep.' But it was Gloria's voice. It was Gloria.

Thursday

Last Words

T HE NEWSPAPER STORY revolved entirely around me and Stephen, but there were seven witnesses: four at the bus stop, two crossing the road, and me. We remained in our separate positions for a long second, staring. Then a woman at the bus-stop took out her mobile and stabbed 999. 'Fire engine, I think,' she snapped, after a short pause. 'And ambulance. All of them. It's an earthquake, or a bomb.' I approached the crater, gingerly. It wasn't an earthquake or a bomb, it was, as far as I could tell, subsidence. The road caved in a little, the bus essentially drove into a big hole. As I watched, bizarrely, the automatic doors hissed open, and a passenger stumbled out. I jumped into the hole to help, which is when I smelt the petrol, then saw it, glugging cheerfully out of the carcass of the bus.

'Get out, quick, the petrol's leaking!'

Probably I should have been calm and reassuring, but I wasn't.

'Come on, get a move on!'

I hectored. I stood at the door like an impatient ticket collector as confused passengers emerged, hurrying them, directing them towards others now standing at the edge of the hole.

There was a weak voice from inside the bus. 'I need a hand.' It quavered, it sounded lonely and uncertain of receiving a reply. It was Stephen.

I peered in. It was dark in the bus and the floor tipped downwards. There was the smell of dry earth and there was the wet, floral aroma of petrol vapour. If anyone standing above us lit a match, there might be an explosion. If the bus stirred and a spark flew, there might be an explosion. Stupidly, I remembered my words, late on Saturday night in a street in Bradford. *Maybe Max had the right idea.* Maybe he didn't. I climbed into the bus.

Stephen was behind the driver's seat. He was holding the seat with one hand and his head with the other. He was swaying.

'Stephen.'

He turned his head to me slowly, as if he was underwater. Bleared at me a moment. 'Are you all right?' he slurred.

I laughed. I didn't mean to, but I couldn't help it. He looked away from me, crossly I thought, but then I followed his gaze and saw the driver, bent over shards of windscreen.

'We should leave him,' I said. 'Shouldn't move him.'

'He might be bleeding,' said Stephen.

'You go,' I said. 'Get help.'

I edged past him, lowering myself down the sloping floor towards the driver. I didn't want to move him. He might have a broken arm and he'd scream if I touched it. He might have a broken neck and I could end up paralysing him. I didn't want to move him, but his green jacket was darkening as blood spread through it.

'His jacket,' said Stephen.

'Yeah, thanks, I can see.'

Stephen interfering as usual, getting in the way as usual. I got hold of the driver's shoulders and pulled him back. He was flexible and unresisting but heavy as a sandbag. He was still wearing sunglasses, but his mouth flopped open and he drooled, so he didn't look cool. He said 'Wha?' I said, 'Don't worry, it's all right.' I didn't know if it was all right, but his body wasn't inclining at any odd angles, so I hoped nothing major was broken. Stephen took an arm. I'd been thinking we'd wait now, but I didn't argue, I took an arm too, and we dragged him out. I was glad of the physical exercise because I was starting to shake. How could the world ever seem safe again, when the ground just opens up and swallows a bus? What's happening to the world? Perhaps the mass effort of faith we all make is fraying. We got the driver out and I was going to say something to Stephen along these lines: *Do you think the mass effort of faith we all make is fraying?* But flash bulbs went off, distracting me, and then Stephen fainted.

So that happened. Then Stephen half woke up in hospital, mistook me for a nurse and was rude about me, and I booked an extra night at the B&B. Chatted to the couple with the baby over breakfast, who'd seen my picture in the local paper. Turned out her brother works in Hong Kong. She gave me her number. Another two potential English friends. I was modest about the headline, the story, the interview. It was nothing. Anyone would have done the same. (*Except they didn't*, I was thinking, *they all stood there gaping while I did something*.)

Preparing to see him again, I chose black. Surely he couldn't mistake a black T-shirt for a nurse's uniform. Perhaps though I should stick to pale blue, see if I could tease some more confessions out of him. I chose black and made a parcel, like a picnic with extras. Sandwiches, drinks, fruit, the newspaper, the letters (stolen from his pocket), and Max's box. Then I made a phone call using his mobile, which I'd also stolen, or borrowed, from his pocket. It was a lengthy phone call, and awkward in places, but it was successful. Then I went to the hospital.

He was on a four-bed ward. Sitting up and looking around, but diminished by his surroundings. I remembered my first sight of him—skinny, pasty-faced teacher with dark rings round his eyes. He still looked dazed, I wasn't sure how much he was taking in. 'Subsidence.' I thought if I repeated it enough, it should sink in. 'The road just gave way. The driver's all right. No one was much hurt. It was subsidence.'

'Still.'

'I know. One minute you're on a bus, the next it's like *The Poseidon Adventure.*'

'It's hazy,' he said. 'Did you laugh at me?'

A week's gone by, and we've hardly exchanged a kind word. I told him it was a nervous laugh, and not to be so sensitive. I unfolded the newspaper and asked him, did he realise we were heroes?

ANGELS OF MERCY. The headline blared above a large picture of me dazzled by the flash, and Stephen on the point of fainting, carrying the slumped driver between us. Stephen was described as a local man, and I was described as his close friend, who has family connections to Scarborough. I sat on his bed and we ate the sandwiches and drank the juice, while we read the piece and the short interview I'd given. (I told them: 'It was nothing. Anyone would have done the same.' But in their story I said: 'Yes I was scared, but I knew someone had to act. That bus could have turned into a fireball.')

When we'd finished reading we talked more about the incident than it deserved, putting off more difficult subjects. It was what we'd been doing all week, using stories both to communicate and to fend each other off. There was a pause, finally. Stephen sitting up in bed, me cross-legged on the mattress.

'I can go, soon as the doctor's looked at me,' he said.

'I know. And there's somewhere I want to take you.'

'Where?'

'Wait and see.'

We didn't talk then about what he'd said, when he thought I was a nurse. We didn't talk about him sending Greg and Robbie and James out looking for me. We didn't talk about what I'd written and he'd found, suggesting to him that I needed saving. Perhaps we would in the future. There was no rush.

I took out Max's box. 'He meant us to force it,' I said. 'There's no secret catch, or hidden key, or clever mechanism. We have to break it open. It's just a question of having the guts to do it.'

He took the box from me, turned it over, turned it round. 'OK,' he said. 'And I think I know who the letters are from.'

'I think I know too.'

We let that moment stretch. It was a space to rest in, after our eventful week, as if the ward was a place for both of us to recover, before the next thing. Before leaving the hospital, opening the box, talking about the letters, before leaving Scarborough and re-entering our lives. A nurse came and took Stephen's temperature, blood pressure, pulse. A doctor followed, looked at the results, looked into his eyes, spoke to him briefly and told him he was fine, he could go home, he was fine.

'I have a story about boxes,' I said, as he got dressed. 'It's a story about a severed head in a box. A friend of mine knows someone in Hong Kong who's in a gang. Some sort of mob thing.'

Stephen looked at me as he pulled up his trousers. 'What are you talking about?'

'I'm talking about this guy who got killed. What he did was, he said something he shouldn't have said. Something disrespectful to one of his superiors. Anyway, he had to die. The killers came to his flat above a grocer's, and they brought a box which had been full of apples. They killed him, beheaded the corpse, put the head in the empty box and took it to show their boss. So they open the box and the boss looks in and nods, and they're going to close the box again, but then the head opens its eyes. It opens its eyes and speaks.

'It says, "Where am I? What happened to me?"

'The boss is fascinated. He sees an opportunity here. He says to the head, "You're dead. I've always wondered, please tell me, what's death like?"

'The head pauses a minute, like it's thinking it over. Then it says, "Death smells of apples."'

Stephen buttoned his shirt, looked at me suspiciously. 'What's that mean? Is that about Max?'

I smiled. 'It's just a story.'

We drove to the Spa and found a parking place. Stephen said yes, he could manage the climb, the fresh air would be good for him. Colour was coming back to his cheeks, he seemed more alert. We climbed slowly, side by side, up to the viewpoint, pausing only to find a suitable, sharp-edged stone. When we got there, we sat on the ground and rested a while, Stephen leaning against the stone post, me beside him, Max's box between us. I held it one last time, appreciating the craft and the effort it represented. Then I battered it with the stone, aiming at a patch of bare wood within the careful silver pattern till it dented, cracked, and broke. I looked at Stephen, who nodded. I reached in with two fingers, and tweezed out the folded sheet of paper. It was not blank, and it was not a sketch, it was a note. Although Max hadn't even filled the page, his handwriting was so cramped it was hard to read, as if he was working within impossibly narrow lines.

The first five words confirmed what we both already knew.

Did you get my letters?

Max was the only one who could have written them. He was the only one who knew enough and cared enough to have written them. My brother the manipulator, the man who liked the last word. I held the note so that Stephen could see it, but I read it out-loud anyway, imagining Max's voice.

You two, you both hang back, you both turn away. Thought I'd give you something to do together. Because I know where hanging back gets you. Are you wondering why I did it? But you know, don't you? Because I couldn't cope. OK? I mean come on, the bayonet must have been a clue. I couldn't cope, that's all. I have no wise words for you. Try not to die. That's it. Try not to die.

I wanted him to say I love you, you've been a good sister, and I'm sorry. Instead I got a man sunk inside himself, unable to see further than his own stifling mood. For a week I'd been fighting with Stephen over stewardship of Max's memory. Now I felt the need to apologise for him.

'This is unworthy of him,' I said.

Stephen stared at me, and I stared at him. Max and his everlasting silence present in the heavy silent moment between us.

Stephen felt he'd had a near-death experience. He felt Gloria had been skating pretty close to death too. He blamed Max. Max the bastard, with his stupid games, trying to remain present in their lives after he'd chosen to leave them. Gloria got out the letters, and puzzled over them, as he had on the train. A literary critic examining a text, finding the hidden meaning, the submerged pattern, the stylistic nuance.

Stephen didn't watch. He looked away, over the town, the busy beach, and out to sea. Children's screams and parents' shouts were carried up to them as wordless sounds, like the squealing of the gulls. Gloria was still reading. He watched the sluggish clouds, drifting aimlessly across the sky. Still reading. This was worse than waiting for the doctor to pronounce on him. What was she going to deduce from her brother's words? She finally looked up, ready with her diagnosis.

Stephen lifted a finger.

'Just a minute. We're at the end of a long week and we've said a lot of things and I'd like, if it's all right with you, to do something tactile.'

'Sorry?'

'I thought we might want . . .'

'Yes, I understood, I just didn't think it needed nego-tiating.'

They embraced. Leant towards each other, put their arms around each other, and hugged. One of her hands sliding up and down his back a little, one of his gently patting her shoulder. He kissed her cheek, scraping it with his two-day-old stubble. 'Sorry about Max,' he said, quietly, near her ear, as if this was a secret to be passed between them. 'He was a bastard, wasn't he, but we both loved him all the same.' Her hand found his shoulder and squeezed it tightly. Then they disentangled and he lay back and waited for her conclusions.

She wiped her eyes and sighed. 'This is what I get from these,' she said, tapping the letters on her knee. 'He knew you'd say it wasn't suicide. He thought you hadn't engaged with how he felt. He didn't think we'd get on. He thought we were both in danger of idolising him. He wants you and Rachel to get back together.'

Stephen lifted himself up on one elbow. 'Hang on, how do you work that out?'

'Which part?'

'Rachel.'

'Who do you think sent these, Stephen?'

He sat up. Gloria continued.

'She told me she had no idea Max was going to kill himself. After he died she went ahead and posted them, because it was his last request. She was going to tell you.'

He sat up, hardly listening, thinking of Rachel. Rachel, passionate and hurt and still, as far as he could see, in love. Unaccountably. He took a long breath of grass-scented air. 'I think my head's clearing,' he said. 'I think I'm waking up.'

He sat up, took the breath, said he was waking up, all with a picture of Rachel in his head, and then she appeared, her hair, her face, the rest of her, up the path behind Gloria, who was smiling at him, affectionate and amused.

So that went rather well. Rachel had been dubious when I called her, but I'd told her two things: that we knew she was sending Max's letters, and that Stephen hadn't stopped thinking about her since we'd all met on Monday. They were partial truths. Seems Max's talent for manipulation runs in the family, and Stephen isn't the only one who can arrange meetings. Rachel said he must be furious, I told her he wanted to talk to her.

She came up the path. Stephen was looking dazed again. We arranged to meet later, Rachel gave me a quick, surprising hug and then I left them to it. I headed down the hill to find an Internet café, looking at the letter she had surreptitiously passed me. An envelope, my name on it, scrawled not in some anonymous typeface, but in Max's distinctive handwriting.

Mochaccino. I put my mug down next to my brother's envelope and read another email from Clara. The smell of chocolate and coffee comforting, like her words. She was all questions at first. *What, forgotten me already?* She wanted to know how I was, what was happening, why no more news from me. *I'm coming home*, she said, *what are you doing? Back to HK? What are you doing?* I took a sip from my mug. I was keen to read the letter of course, to see what else Max had to say. I even lifted the envelope to my face, smelt it, put it in front of my mouth and, with a little glance to right and left, kissed it. But it felt important to speak to the living, not the dead, so I began an email to Clara. I told her I was considering a welcome home party for her, something involving all my English friends, with plenty of opportunities for humans to meet. And then I told her the story of my week, or a story of my week.